It is said, and I believe truly said, that no one of the jungle has ever entered that volcano and returned to tell the tale. . . . It is a place of death, a place of sacrifice.

So it was that people spoke of the mysteries of THE VEILED LADY. Yet, when a beautiful and determined young biologist disappears beneath the mists of the forbidden volcano, the PHANTOM sets out to save her.

THE GHOST WHO WALKS is confronted by the dual challenges of human greed and unimaginable natural threats.

Other Adventures of The Phantom from Avon Books

The Story of THE PHANTOM

THE VEILED LADY

LEE FALK's original story
adapted by Frank S. Shawn

Co-published by Avon Books and
King Features Syndicate

AVON
PUBLISHERS OF BARD, CAMELOT, DISCUS, EQUINOX AND FLARE BOOKS

This Avon edition is the first publication
of *THE VEILED LADY* in book form.

AVON BOOKS
A division of
The Hearst Corporation
959 Eighth Avenue
New York, New York 10019

First Avon Printing, March, 1973.

AVON TRADEMARK REG. U.S. PAT. OFF. AND
FOREIGN COUNTRIES, REGISTERED TRADEMARK—
MARCA REGISTRADA, HECHO EN CHICAGO, U.S.A.

Printed in the U.S.A.

AUTHOR'S NOTE

Old friends of the PHANTOM adventure strip may be interested in knowing more about this series of new novels with the general title "The Story of the Phantom."

All are based on my original stories. I wrote "The Ghost Who Walks." The second and third books, "The Slave Market Of Mucar," and "The Scorpia Menace" were adapted by Basil Copper. "The Veiled Lady" and "The Golden Circle" were adapted by Frank S. Shawn. I wrote the sixth of the series, "The Mysterious Ambassador."

Lee Falk

PROLOGUE

HOW IT ALL BEGAN

Over four hundred years ago, a large British merchant ship was attacked by Singg pirates off the remote shores of Bangalla. The captain of the trading vessel was a famous seafarer who, in his youth, had served as cabin boy to Christopher Columbus on his first voyage to discover the New World. With the captain was his son, Kit, a strong young man who idolized his father and hoped to follow him as a seafarer. But the pirate attack was disastrous. In a furious battle, the entire crew of the merchant ship was killed and the ship sank in flames. The sole survivor was young Kit who, as he fell off the burning ship, saw his father killed by a pirate. Kit was washed ashore, half-dead. Friendly pygmies found him and nursed him to health.

One day, walking on the beach, he found a dead pirate, dressed in his father's clothes. He realized this was the pirate who had killed his father. Grief-stricken, he waited until vultures had stripped the body clean. Then on the skull of his father's murderer, he swore an oath by firelight as the pygmies watched. "I swear to devote my life to the destruction of piracy, greed, cruelty, and injustice—and my sons and their sons shall follow me."

This was the Oath of the Skull that Kit and his descendants would live by. In time, the pygmies led him to their home in the Deep Woods in the center of the jungle, where he found a large cave with many

7

rock-strewn chambers. The mouth of the cave, a natural formation formed by the water and wind of centuries, was curiously like a skull. This became his home, the Skull Cave. He soon adopted a mask and a strange costume. He found that the mystery and fear this inspired helped him in his endless battle against world-wide piracy. For he and his sons who followed became known as the nemesis of pirates everywhere: a mysterious man whose face no one ever saw, whose name no one knew, who worked alone.

As the years passed, he fought injustice wherever he found it. The first Phantom and the sons who followed found their wives in many places. One married a reigning queen, one a princess, one a beautiful red-haired barmaid. But whether queen or commoner, all followed their men back to the Deep Woods to live the strange but happy life of the wife of the Phantom. And of all the world, only she, wife of the Phantom and their children, could see his face.

Generation after generation was conceived and born, grew to manhood, and assumed the tasks of the father before him. Each wore the mask and costume. Folk of the jungle and the city and sea began to whisper that there was a man who could not die, a Phantom, a Ghost Who Walks. For they thought the Phantom was always the same man. A boy who saw the Phantom would see him again fifty years after; and he seemed the same. And he would tell his son and his grandson; and then his son and grandson would see the Phantom fifty years after that. And he would seem the same. So the legend grew. The Man Who Cannot Die. The Ghost Who Walks. The Phantom.

The Phantom did not discourage this belief in his immortality. Always working alone against tremendous—sometimes almost impossible—odds, he found

8

that the awe and fear the legend inspired was a great help in his endless battle against evil. Only his friends, the pygmies, knew the truth. To compensate for their tiny stature, the pygmies, mixed deadly poisons for use on their weapons in hunting or defending themselves. It was rare that they were forced to defend themselves. Their deadly poisons were known through the jungle, and they and their home, the Deep Woods, were dreaded and avoided. Another reason to stay away from the Deep Woods—it soon became known that this was a home of the Phantom, and none wished to trespass.

Through the ages, the Phantoms created several more homes, or hideouts, in various parts of the world. Near the Deep Woods was the Isle of Eden, where the Phantom taught all animals to live in peace. In the southwest desert of the New World, the Phantoms created an eyrie on a high, steep mesa that was thought by the Indians to be haunted by evil spirits and became known as "Walker's Table"—for the Ghost Who Walks. In Europe, deep in the crumbling cellars of ancient castle ruins, the Phantom had another hideout from which to strike against evildoers.

But the Skull Cave in the quiet of the Deep Woods remained the true home of the Phantom. Here, in a rocky chamber, he kept his chronicles, the written records of all his adventures. Phantom after Phantom faithfully wrote their experiences in the large folio volumes. Another chamber contained the costumes of all the generations of Phantoms. Other chambers contained the vast treasures of the Phantom acquired over the centuries, used only in the endless battle against evil.

Thus, twenty generations of Phantoms lived, fought, and died—usually violently—as they fulfilled their oath. Jungle folk, sea folk and city folk believed him the same man, the Man Who Cannot Die. Only the pygmies knew that always a day would come when their great friend would die. Then, alone, a strong young son would carry his father to the burial crypt of his ancestors, where all Phantoms rested. As the pygmies waited outside, the young man would emerge from the cave, wearing the mask, the costume, and the skull ring of the Phantom; his carefree, happy days as the Phantom's son were over. And the pygmies would chant their age-old chant, "The Phantom is dead. Long live the Phantom."

This story of The Veiled Lady is an adventure of the Phantom of our time—the twenty-first generation of his line. He has inherited the traditions and responsibilities created by four centuries of Phantom ancestors. One ancestor created the Jungle Patrol. Thus, today, our Phantom is the mysterious and unknown commander of this elite corps. In the jungle, he is known and loved as the keeper of the peace. On his right hand is the Skull Ring that leaves his mark —the Sign of the Skull—known and feared by evildoers everywhere. On his left hand—closer to the heart—is his "good mark" ring. Once given, the mark grants the lucky bearer protection by the Phantom, and it is equally known and respected. And to good people and criminals alike, in the jungle, on the seven seas, and in the cities of the world, he is the Phantom, the Ghost Who Walks, the Man Who Cannot Die.

Lee Falk
New York 1972

P.S. Readers of this continuing series should be advised that on the title page of THE SLAVE MARKET OF MUCAR, Phantom #2, the name of the adaptor, Basil Copper, was inadvertently omitted.

CHAPTER ONE

They saw her first when they were several thousand feet in the air.

The pilot of the Bangalla Airways jet introduced them. "On our left, ladies and gentlemen, one of the world's largest volcanoes," he announced over the intercom. "She's known around here as the Veiled Lady."

Most of the jet passengers obligingly looked. They were nearly to their destination of Mawitaan, the capital city of Bangalla, and a little less awed by the natural wonders of the dark continent than they had been when their flight began a few hours ago. They were preoccupied now with the imminent landing, with thinking about gathering their luggage once they were on the ground, and with getting to their hotels.

Two passengers, though, seemed more than casually interested in the great mist-shrouded volcano. One was a lovely blonde girl in her late twenties. She was tall, suntanned, dressed in a simple denim skirt and a checked blouse. A notebook, with a pocked black-leather cover, lay open on her lap. "Well, Karl, there she is," the girl said to her companion with a pleased smile.

"Just as aloof and mysterious as advertised," said the young man in the seat beside her. He was over six feet in height, wide-shouldered, with a sun-and-wind-weathered face. His light hair and short, cropped beard were bleached by much outdoor life.

11

"The volcano is called the Veiled Lady," continued the pilot, "because of the perpetual clouds at her summit. That misty veil is said to be caused by rising columns of hot air. She's supposed to be inactive, but one never knows."

The slender blonde girl jotted something in her open notebook.

The pilot added, "The sides of the volcano are so steep no one has ever been able to climb down. No one has ever seen the bottom."

The blonde girl squeezed the arm of her companion. "Until now," she said in a quiet voice.

Outside the port-city airport, the afternoon glared hot and dry. The sky was a hot blue color; the distant hills flickered in a warm haze. Inside, however, there was a pleasant chill.

In the reception room, a plump weary-looking Chinese of about thirty-five sat slouched in a brittle blue-plastic chair. He was listening and watching, a small sad smile on his face.

As he sat slumped in the air-conditioned room, he rolled himself, slowly and patiently, thick homemade cigarettes. When the flight was announced, the Chinese straightened somewhat in his chair. He lit the latest of his hand-rolled cigarettes with a wooden match, his tired smile broadening.

His name was Tinn. Right now, there were two things he was predominantly interested in. One was the misty volcano called the Veiled Lady. The other was the lovely tanned blonde whose jet was landing outside in the bright, glaring afternoon.

Below, and to the right, the waters of Mawitaan Bay glowed deep blue in the sunlight. The taxicab climbed slowly through the humid streets.

12

The pretty blonde girl slapped her notebook shut, leaned back, and expelled a breath upward out of her mouth. "I really think I must be suffering from jet shock or whatever they call it," she said, smiling across at her bearded companion. "I mean I still don't quite believe we're here, that this is Mawitaan." She tilted one hand toward the open window of the slowly climbing cab.

The glaring street was thick with life. European and American styles of dress mixed with the native fashions of Bangalla to form a patchwork of colors. The most modern and up-to-date businesses rubbed shoulders with the most ancient; slick, leather briefcases were as frequent as straw baskets; men talked anxiously of stocks and bonds while others sold fresh fruit on the street corners.

"Maybe you feel," said the young man with the weather-bleached beard, "we should still be back home pulling strings and filling out forms."

The girl said, "This little pilgrimage to the Veiled Lady did seem to involve us in a lot more red tape than usual."

"Probably because money isn't as easy these days as it was for our other excursions."

The girl ceased smiling, pressing her lips tightly together. Finally, she said, "But, darn it, Karl, this is the most important thing I've ever done. That's what I tried to explain to those fuddy-duddies back in Boston."

Karl laughed. "Relax. You convinced them well enough and we're here."

The girl smiled once again. "Yes, we are. And I've got a feeling."

"Feeling about what?"

"I've got a feeling we're going to find even more than we expect," she said. "Yes, much more."

The Scarlet Cockatoo Café stood on a narrow street

13

near the Mawitaan harbor. The smell of the sea was strong here, mixed with the scent of cargoes from all over the world—spices, foodstuffs, produce, machinery.

Dark women in loose, full-length dresses of bright yellow and red moved along the twisting street, some with huge wicker baskets balanced on their heads.

Tinn, the plump weary Chinese, came ambling along the hot sidewalk, puffing on a fat brown cigarette. His wrinkled suit was a faded blue and he looked almost colorless as he walked among the women in their brilliant stripes and flower patterns.

Tinn pushed the thick oaken door of the Scarlet Cockatoo open. A shadowy coolness surrounded him once he was across the threshold. There were only a few customers; the hum of the big overhead fans was louder than any of the conversations.

The tired-looking Chinese stopped at the long black bar long enough to stub out his cigarette in a shell ashtray. The five caged birds hanging up behind the bar hopped and cawed.

Beyond the beaded archway stretched a gray corridor. Tinn trotted to the corridor's end and tapped three times on another heavy oak door. "It's me."

"Come in, come in," said a thin raspy voice. "I could smell that tobacco of yours a block away, Tinn. When are you going to give up smoking?"

Tinn smiled sadly at the soft-looking fat man seated on a wicker sofa at the far end of the large, cool office. "It helps pass the time," he explained. "I have to sit and wait a good deal, Mr. Barber."

Barber was forty-one years old, a loose, sprawling man in black clothes. His skin was pale white and he had a fuzzy circle of beard surrounding his small mouth. "Well, it's your health you're jeopardizing."

"I hear extra weight isn't so good for the health,

14

either." Tinn slumped into a canvas butterfly chair, smiling wearily.

Barber's left eye narrowed. He watched the Chinese for several seconds before asking, "All right, what about those two?"

"They arrived half an hour ago by Bangalla Airways jet," replied Tinn. "Just as we were informed."

Barber steepled his soft plump fingers together, resting his notched chin on them. A faint wheeze commenced in his vast chest. "They really plan to do this thing?"

"Oh, yes," replied the Chinese. "I managed to stand quite near while they retrieved their suitcases and equipment. It was all the girl could talk about."

"Going down into the Veiled Lady," said Barber, his little blue eyes half-closing, "right to the very bottom. It takes considerable nerve."

"Certain worthwhile objectives," observed Tinn, "give people nerve."

"Money," said Barber. "The possibility of turning up a good deal of money—that's what makes everything go around." His little eyes closed completely as he sighed. "Are they staying at the Mawitaan Plaza Hotel?"

"Yes, that's what they told the taxidriver."

Barber's large pale head bobbed several times. "Good, good," he said, a louder wheeze escaping from his little mouth. "Now I have to set certain other operations in motion." He made a dismissing gesture with one fat hand.

"And me?"

"Get back to watching them," ordered Barber.

"Okay." Tinn smiled sadly and stood up. His right hand sank into his coat pocket, closing around his tobacco pouch.

CHAPTER TWO

Sergeant Barnum of the Jungle Patrol was shooting at his toes.

He'd swung his swivel chair over closer to the air-conditioning outlet and thrust his big booted feet up on his wooden desk. Carefully, with a look of deep concentration on his broad sunburned face, the squat sergeant was shooting paper clips at his feet with a rubber band. "Big toe, left foot," he said, letting fly a shiny silver clip.

"Bull's-eye," said the slender blonde girl who stepped into Jungle Patrol headquarters out of the hot afternoon.

"Oops." Sergeant Barnum swung his feet hurriedly off the desk, almost sending his in/out box sailing over the edge. He got himself upright, and touched his low wide forehead in an informal salute. "Good afternoon, miss. What can we do for you?"

The tall bearded man who'd been with the girl on the plane followed her into the JP outer office now. "We have an appointment with Colonel Weeks. Doctor Love of Boston University."

Barnum's thick shaggy eyebrows nearly touched as he frowned. "Oh, sure. About the Veiled Lady business." Moving toward the door of the colonel's office, he said, "Boy, I wouldn't want to try to climb down into that baby for love or money—or both."

The Jungle Patrol was the major peace-keeping body in the Bangalla area. The patrol operated on the

16

jungle borders and the no-man's land between the small countries along a thousand-mile border. It was an elite corps. Of the thousands of men of all races from all over the world who applied each year, only a few, after undertaking rigorous tests, were accepted.

Colonel Weeks, the commanding officer of the Jungle Patrol, was a large, gray-haired man. He was sitting behind his wide gray-metal desk, which he liked to keep as uncluttered as possible, puffing on his pipe when Sergeant Barnum knocked and stepped in. "Is that a rubber band around your forefinger, Sergeant?" asked the colonel.

"Oops." The squat Sergeant Barnum frowned at his forefinger, and put his hand behind his back. "That's right, sir, and you have suggested I refrain from practicing my marksmanship out in my cubbyhole. Sorry, sir."

The colonel nodded, waiting for the sergeant to get to the business which had brought him.

"They're here," announced Sergeant Barnum.

Exhaling pipe smoke, the gray-haired colonel asked, "Who would *they* be, Sergeant?"

"That Doctor Love who wants to jump into the volcano," explained the chunky sergeant. "And, Colonel, you ought to see the terrific blonde he's got with——"

"If you'll show them in, I can get a look at both of them."

"Oh, sure, right. Yes, sir."

The colonel stood, resting his pipe in the dark stone ashtray at the side of his desk, as the slim blonde and her tall, bearded companion entered his office. "Good afternoon," he said. After smiling at both of them, Colonel Weeks crossed to the rear window of his office. He ran a finger along the bamboo slats of the

17

curtain. The sound of rifle fire drifted from the target range. "Let me get to the point at once. No one has ever survived an attempt to climb down into that volcano." He turned to face the two. "The sides are much too steep and——"

"We know that," said the bearded young man. "We plan to fly down by copter. We've already made arrangements to hire——"

"Suicide. With the quirky air currents inside the Veiled Lady and lord knows what other dangers . . . it's suicide." Colonel Weeks strode up to the young man. "I think, Doctor Love, you're a fool to think of risking not only your neck but that of this fragile young woman here."

The girl laughed. "I'm Doctor Love, Colonel."

"Good Lord! You mean this expedition is being headed by a. . . ." began the surprised colonel. He got hold of himself and removed the stunned look from his weathered face.

"Yes, Colonel—by a woman." The girl was sitting in one of the rattan visitors' chairs, her long slim legs crossed, her black notebook resting on one knee. "Doctor Jan Love, professor of biology at Boston University. This is Doctor Karl Waagener, an associate professor in our department."

From the outer office, from the vicinity of Sergeant Barnum's desk, came a sound that was somewhere between an exclamation and a snort. "A lady boss," the sergeant muttered to himself.

Before he said anything further, the colonel went back behind his desk. He picked up his pipe and bit down on the stem. "I see," he said finally. He opened a crisp manila folder, thumbed through the papers inside. "You say you wish to explore the volcano because——?"

"From what we've heard there may be many interesting life-forms down there," said Doctor Jan Love. "The odd conditions that exist within the volcano, the continual steam, and the complete isolation from the outside world for centuries, perhaps for thousands of years." The slender girl had uncrossed her legs and was leaning forward in her chair, her eyes glowing. "Going down there is like, well, like going back to the dawn of time, to the beginning of things. In a way, Colonel, I feel like Darwin must have felt when he came near the Galápagos archipelago. You know, the United States and Russia have been exploring the moon and even Mars. To me, well, your Veiled Lady is as big a challenge as the moon or Mars and she may provide us with more answers as to what life is all about than all the space probes put——" The pretty scientist stopped, laughed. "Excuse me, Colonel, for giving you a biology lecture. I simply want to convince you that, as a biologist, I'm dying to explore the Veiled Lady. On top of which I really think it would be a heck of a lot of fun."

The colonel went back to studying the papers in the folder for a moment. "I should have done my homework on you, Doctor. I see by these letters that you have a considerable reputation in your field." He leaned back in his chair, blowing smoke toward the ceiling. "I suppose you've heard the other stories about our Veiled Lady?"

Karl said, "If you think we came to search for the mysterious treasure of the Veiled Lady, Colonel, let me put your mind at ease. We don't believe in such nonsense."

"Many people do, however," the colonel told them. "Which is one reason I know how treacherous the Veiled Lady is. Dangerous and difficult for the best of men. Two parties in the past decade have made a try for that treasure. No one ever returned from either attempt."

"We're not anthropologists or folklore collectors," said the slender blonde girl. "We're only interested in what really may exist in the volcano, in life-forms we can study and classify. The legends about sacrifices of maidens and gold and jewels in the dim past don't interest us at all."

Gesturing at the file in Colonel Weeks's hands, Karl said, "You'll notice Jan has been in a good many rough and out-of-the-way places, Colonel. She's never let the real hazards of a place get the best of her. She's certainly never been much worried about local superstitions."

Jan Love said, "If I start believing in the legend of a fabulous treasure, I may even come to believe in this jungle bogey man of yours."

"In what?" asked Colonel Weeks.

"In the legend of this undying mystery man who skulks around the jungle," said Jan. "What is it they call him? The Phantom?"

"Yes, the Phantom," said Karl. "You find similar naive beliefs in many parts of the world."

The colonel watched both of them for a moment before he grinned. "No doubt," he said, closing the file. After clearing his throat, he continued, "I'm in sympathy with your intentions, Doctor Love. However, I'm very much afraid I can't allow you to explore the Veiled Lady."

Karl half-rose out of his chair. "You mean you'll try to prevent us from flying into that volcano?"

"Yes. The Jungle Patrol has all the licensing authority for the area," the colonel pointed out. "I'm refusing permission. Sorry."

Jan ran a finger along her cheek. "I think I know why, Colonel."

"Oh, so?"

"It's because I'm a woman, isn't it?"

Colonel Weeks cleared his throat once more. "Well, yes, in a way. I'm really thinking of your safety, Doctor Love. The Veiled Lady is too dangerous—much too dangerous—for a girl."

"Yes, I've heard that before." Jan left her chair, and moved to face the colonel across his desk. "If I were a man then, you'd permit us to fly into the volcano?"

"Well," said the colonel, meeting the lovely biologist's eyes. "I'd still advise against it, but, yes, the license would be granted."

There was a silence and in it they all heard the crack of shots out on the rifle range.

"Suppose," said Jan suddenly, "I prove I'm as capable as the average man of taking care of myself. Will you give us the darn license then?"

"I hadn't thought of putting you to a test, Doctor Love," said Colonel Weeks, grinning, a little puzzled. "However, I suppose I'm open to being convinced. What exactly did you have in mind?"

Jan straightened, jerked a thumb at the window. "Let's go outside. I'll show you, Colonel."

The slender blonde girl removed a thick rubber band from between the pages of her black notebook. After tossing the notebook to Karl, she pulled back her hair and used the elastic to hold it in place. "Okay," she announced, "I'll take my turn now if I may."

They were standing out in the hot afternoon, at the shooting end of the Jungle Patrol target range. Dry, brown scrub grass grew around the fenced-in area and some kind of tiny imperturbable insects hovered in the air all about.

The half-dozen young recruits who'd been using the range stood in a semi-circle a short distance from Jan, Karl, and the commander. They were watching the girl, and talking among themselves.

Down at the rack end of the range, a brown, balding Jungle Patrol corporal was tacking up fresh targets. When he had finished he crunched away off the gravel, then waved a hand at the colonel.

Colonel Weeks had let his pipe go out. "All ready for you, Doctor Love." Relighting the pipe, he nodded at one of the young recruits. "Private Reisberson, if you'd be so kind as to loan this young lady your rifle."

"Uh," said the surprised Reisberson, "yes, sir. Here you go, ma'm. Careful you don't. . . ."

The girl handled the rifle expertly. "Still using the M-1 out here, Colonel?" Not waiting for a reply, the blonde stepped to the firing line, which put her a hundred yards from the targets. "Offhand position, first," she said, with the stock against her shoulder, her right hand around the grip and the fingers of her left hand forked just ahead of the balance point. She took a deep breath, held it, and squeezed the trigger.

"Um," remarked Private Reisberson as Jan continued to shoot. "Doggone, look at that."

After firing ten shots, Jan lowered the borrowed rifle.

In a moment, the balding corporal came trotting up to them, waving the target the girl had used. "You better sign her up, Colonel."

The Jungle Patrol commander took the target. "Well, well," he said. Nothing much was left of the bull's-eye of the decimal target. Eight of Jan's shots had hit the ten spot and the other two had penetrated the nine circle next to it.

"Shall we try it from a kneeling position next?" asked the smiling Jan.

The colonel held the riddled target up between himself and the bright sun. "I don't think that will be necessary, Doctor."

The girl shrugged. "Just when I was getting warmed up." She returned the rifle to Private Reisberson.

"Um, doggone," he said.

Hands on hips, Jan was surveying the Jungle Patrol grounds. "Stables over there and then the gym up on that little rise, right?"

"Yes," said the colonel.

"Let's visit the stables next," Jan said.

Karl put his arm around her shoulders and the two of them started off.

After a second, the colonel followed.

A little over an hour and a half later Sergeant Barnum rolled forward in his chair, dropped his rubber bands and a handful of paper clips back in the drawer. He went and looked into his commanding officer's office. The door had stood open for the past fifteen minutes. "It's quitting time and . . . you look a little odd, sir."

"Well, I feel a little odd, Sergeant," admitted the colonel, rubbing at his left arm.

"I heard you giving those two scientists a license to explore the Veiled Lady," said Sergeant Barnum. "I thought you didn't believe in ladies doing dangerous stuff like that."

"Doctor Love isn't exactly your ordinary everyday

23

lady." The colonel shifted in his chair, rubbing again at his arm.

"What were you all up to outside?"

"Well, Sergeant, the young lady was demonstrating to me that my ideas about her were merely male chauvinist notions with little or no basis in reality."

"Oh, yeah? How'd she do that?"

The colonel nodded toward the window, then winced. "First she stepped onto the rifle range and hit eight out of ten bull's-eyes."

"Hey, that's not bad."

"Not at all," agreed Colonel Weeks. "Then she visited the stables, saddled and mounted one of our meanest horses, and took him over all the hurdles and hazards. After which, our Doctor Love dropped in at the gym and bested every man there in judo. She even threw our top man on his ear."

Sergeant Barnum blinked. "I thought you were the JP's top judo man, sir."

"So did I." The colonel picked up his pipe with his sore arm and lit it. "That will be all for today, Sergeant."

"It's enough." Sergeant Barnum saluted and left the colonel alone with his thoughts.

CHAPTER THREE

A soft, warm rain had just stopped. The sun showed up again in the morning sky and fuzzy rainbows flashed in the small oily puddles at the edge of the private airfield. A soot-colored dog hobbled out of the rain-dotted brush beyond the field, came up, and sniffed at a pool of bright water. The dog suddenly cocked its head and hastened back into the brush.

Through the gate in the airfield's cyclone fence a bright-orange compact car, rich with dents and scratches, came rattling. It swayed, squealed a little, changed its course, and came to a halt in a narrow parking area beside a low building with a red-tile roof. After the orange car stopped, it continued rattling for another ten seconds, then gave an explosive gasp and became still.

A big black man in a yellow-and-green dashiki hopped from the driver's seat, beckoning the other two people in the vehicle to disembark. "Safe and sound, right on time," he announced, readjusting his taxidriver's cap.

Tiny birds, whose colors matched the cabdriver's pullover, went fluttering up out of the dozen or so trees bordering the airfield's office building. Off in the brush, the sooty dog barked twice.

Karl Waagener stepped out of the battered cab, grinning. He held out his hand to Jan Love. "I can see what Colonel Weeks meant about this being a dangerous mission," he said. "I didn't think we'd survive this cab ride to our copter field."

Jan had her long blonde hair tied back with a dark ribbon. She wore an olive-tinted pair of aviator-style sunglasses, khaki slacks, and a blouse. "He's not a bad driver actually, only a bit too enthusiastic."

The cab driver unstrapped their luggage from the roof of his orange car. Walking around the cab with some of the bags, he stopped. "That's interesting," he observed. "Lost another fender. Huh."

"I think it was when we went up on the sidewalk to avoid the fruit vendor's bicycle," said Karl, handing more of their equipment down.

Jan said, "I bet it was when we sideswiped that herd of goats on the outskirts of Mawitaan."

The driver shook his head. "I think not, miss. I've sideswiped a good many goats in my day and never lost a fender that way yet." He shrugged. "Well, back to business." After setting their equipment, packs, and luggage on the mosaic tile steps of the airfield office, he told Karl what the fare was.

Jan paid him, adding an extra bill. "And something toward a new fender." She made a note of the amount in her notebook.

Taking the cash, the driver walked toward his cab. "Allow me to wish you good luck," he said. "From what I overheard of your plans while we drove out here, I'd say you'll need a good deal of luck. The Veiled Lady, huh?" He jumped into the orange machine and went rattling away.

As the cab shot out through the gate, a jeep came driving in.

Jan, recognizing the colors and insignia of the Jungle Patrol, said, "Don't tell me Colonel Weeks has had second thoughts about our license to explore the Veiled Lady."

Karl patted the pocket of his tan bushjacket. "Too late. We've got all the official papers we need for our jaunt."

The tiny yellow-and-green birds had returned to roost in the trees. They scattered away into the clear morning air once more.

Sergeant Barnum parked the JP jeep where the cab had been, turned off the ignition, and wiped at his broad sunburned face with the freckled back of his hand. He smiled over at Doctors Jan Love and Karl Waagener, giving them a lazy salute.

Colonel Weeks, the tall, gray-haired commander of the Jungle Patrol, stepped out of the jeep and came striding over. "I decided to see you off."

"And maybe talk us out of the whole darn thing," said Jan, smiling at the straight-backed colonel.

"I know you can handle yourself in ordinary tough situations, Doctor Love. You've proven that," said the colonel. "What worries me is the fact that things may be far from ordinary down inside the volcano. Frankly, I'd suggest——"

"Frankly," cut in Jan, still smiling at the Jungle Patrol commander, "nothing can change my mind. I appreciate your coming to wish us *bon voyage,* Colonel." She reached out to take hold of his rough, weathered hand. "Now, good-bye."

The door of the airfield office opened and a long, lean black man looked out. He wore a striped pullover shirt and faded denim trousers. In a holster at his side was a .38 revolver. "Going along on this excursion, Colonel Weeks?"

The colonel studied the pilot for a few seconds.

"No, Gabe," he said. "Are you going to fly Doctor Love's copter into the Veiled Lady?"

"Yes, sir, I am." Gabe nodded at Jan and Karl. "I'm Gabe McClennan, your pilot for this little excursion. Colonel Weeks and I are old friends, aren't we?"

"In a way," said the gray-haired colonel. "I thought Orlando was scheduled to handle this flight."

"He had a sudden attack of appendicitis," explained Gabe. He'd come out on the tile porch, and leaned back against the office door. "Or so his wife said when she phoned in for him." Gabe laughed. "Personally, I've got a hunch he's afraid of the Veiled Lady. Which is okay by me. I can use the extra pay and those volcano jujus don't bother me none." He pointed at the pile of luggage and equipment. "Let's get that stuff stowed," he said to Karl.

While Karl and the copter pilot walked out to the blue-and-silver helicopter sitting on the field, Jan said to the Jungle Patrol commander: "For an old friend, you didn't seem too cordial to our pilot. Is there something wrong?"

His eyes following Gabe, Colonel Weeks replied, "No, not really. A few years back Gabe was a pretty wild teenager, gave us all a lot of trouble. I have a hunch he may have been involved in a couple of things since then, but there's never been proof." He shook his head and pulled his pipe out of his pocket. "I suppose I ought to give him the benefit of the doubt. As far as I know, he's been clean the past few years and the people here swear by him. He's a very good pilot, nothing to worry about in that department."

Out at the ship Karl turned and waved to Jan. "Time to leave," she said. "Good-bye, Colonel."

"I want you to keep in contact with us by radio

28

from the copter," Colonel Weeks told her. "I've explained all that to Karl."

"If any superstitions rear their ugly heads, I'll give a good yell right into the mike." Jan turned and left the colonel standing on the tile steps.

Slowly the JP commander returned to his jeep. With one foot in the machine, he stopped to watch the girl board the helicopter. "Sergeant," he said.

"Yes, sir?"

"What did Gabe say was wrong with Orlando?"

"His appendix, sir."

The colonel dug the stem of his pipe into his chin. "At the back of my mind, that doesn't quite ring true."

"How come?"

Colonel Weeks frowned and shook his head. "I can't tell you why," he said. "But I have an idea Corporal Gillis might know."

Everyone was aboard the silver-and-blue copter now. Its rotor was commencing to turn slowly, snapping at the air.

"When we get back to headquarters," said the colonel, "tell Gillis I want to talk to him."

"You think there's something fishy going on?"

A popping sound grew out of the airship. It swayed, blowing dust. As the rotor became invisible, the copter rose straight up into the morning.

His hand shading his eyes, Colonel Weeks said, "No, probably not. Well, let's get back to headquarters and the radio room. I want to keep in touch with the doctor." He lowered himself into the jeep seat.

The copter was high above them now. It swung toward the south, toward the Veiled Lady.

Barber nearly filled the little washroom at the rear of his office. He had his soft, slack face near a wall

29

mirror, and was scraping a safety razor over his lathered cheeks. "Well?" he said out to Tinn.

The weary-looking Chinese was settling into a canvas butterfly chair. "Somebody send you flowers?"

"It's my shaving lotion," said the fat proprietor of the Scarlet Cockatoo. "Did they leave on schedule?"

Tinn tapped his wristwatch. "Right on schedule," he said. "I watched the actual takeoff from the brush behind the field."

"Couldn't you use the office?"

"I didn't want Colonel Weeks to notice me," answered Tinn, slouching further into the wing chair.

"Ouch." A speck of blood showed in the white foam on Barber's left cheek. "What was Colonel Weeks doing at the field?"

"Came to see the girl and her associate off, I assume," said Tinn. "He didn't seem to be upset about anything, although he looked at Gabe funny for a minute there."

Barber held a hot washcloth against his flabby cheek. "We needn't worry about Weeks. He'll be staying here in Mawitaan behind a desk." He dropped the cloth into the basin, and returned to his shaving. "No, things are going quite well. I'm certain Dr. Love knows what's down in that volcano. All this bull about biological wonders is nothing more than a clever cover story, something to fool feeble-minded bureaucrats like Colonel Weeks." He finished shaving, and washed his face. "And what Doctor Love finds will become ours. Yes, things are going very well indeed."

The tired-looking Chinese rubbed a thumb over an insect bite on his wrist. "What about the Phantom?"

"What?" When Barber sat down in his desk chair, all his pores seemed to sigh.

"Do you think Doctor Love will fool the Phantom, too? Do you think she'll be able to haul the——?"

"Look." Barber grabbed a map from his desktop. "This is a map of Bangalla. You'll notice one thing immediately: Bangalla is a big place, mostly wilds and unexplored jungles and forests. I don't care what simple natives may say about the Phantom. That's only a superstition. Even if he existed, there's no way one man can know everything going on around here. Forget the Phantom myth—relax."

Slumped in his chair, Tinn said, "I am relaxed. I merely brought up the topic of the Phantom because. . . ."

"Enough of him." Barber spread the map out and poked at a specific spot with a white pudgy finger. "This is Llongo country."

"Yes," said Tinn. "So?"

"The Llongo tribe lives very close to the Veiled Lady," continued Barber. "You'll be dropped near there this afternoon. You'll join the men I've already got posted in that area. They're lying low in a run-down outpost town. Contact them, then communicate with me. I want to be sure nobody else goes into that volcano—goes in or comes out. And, of course, I want to be notified as soon as there's any word from inside about. . . ."

"I'm an urban person," complained Tinn. "I don't feel good about the idea of going into the jungle."

Barber scowled at him. "Nevertheless, you will go."

"Yes," answered Tinn.

CHAPTER FOUR

Below them now, there was nothing but a matted mass, a thick green tangle stretching out in the afternoon sun. From up in the copter the jungle seemed completely still and silent, a vast patchwork of greens and scarlets and yellows, striped with great bands of deep shadow.

Gradually, the bright colors of leaves and vines and flowers began to blur. Wisps of fine mist were drifting out over the treetops, twisting among the branches.

"There's your famous lady," said Gabe from the pilot's seat. "Coming up ahead."

Jan nodded, not saying anything. She glanced back at Karl, and smiled quietly.

The light of the afternoon grew thinner and hazier. Before them loomed the giant Veiled Lady, her summit shrouded in thick swirls of mist.

The copter rose up, leaving the blurred jungle further below, moving closer to the hollow peak of the ancient volcano.

Jan reached out a slender hand for the radio mike. In a moment, she'd made contact with Jungle Patrol headquarters and Colonel Weeks. "Jan Love here, Colonel Weeks. We're nearly there."

"Listen, Doctor Love," said the colonel, "it's still not too late to turn back." The radio speaker gave his voice a faintly metallic ring. "I really don't think——"

"Colonel, you must know by this time, I have a

distinct stubborn streak," cut in Jan. "I wouldn't stop now for anything. Do you read me? Over."

After a few seconds of silence, the JP commander answered, "Yes. We read you loud and clear, Doctor Love. We've got our tape recorder rolling, so you can start describing what you see as you descend. Over."

"Don't be so glum, Colonel," said Jan. "You sound like you're standing by to record my last words. Over."

"I sincerely hope not. Over."

The jungle had vanished now. There was nothing but thick mist all around their ship.

"Instruments, do your stuff," grinned Gabe, patting the control panel.

The helicopter began swinging gently from side to side, as though it were a pendulum held by a giant hand. The chopping sound of the propeller blades was muffled.

"Hang on, everybody," said Gabe. "I think we're going in."

"Doctor Love, Doctor Love," came the voice of Colonel Weeks. "Are you all right? Please answer. Over."

"Yes, Colonel," replied Jan into the mike, "we're fine. We've just begun our descent into the Veiled Lady. I can't give you much of an idea yet about the old girl since the scenery so far consists of nothing but fog, mist, and more fog."

Gabe began whistling the Gershwin song about a foggy day in London. He was still grinning, but a fine film of perspiration had formed on his forehead.

"We're continuing to drop," Jan went on. "Still nothing much to see. The fog and mist have been joined by steam."

In his seat, to the rear of Jan, Karl was frowning

out at the surrounding whiteness. "That's funny," he said.

Jan glanced back. "What is it, Karl?"

Karl narrowed his left eye, then shook his head. "Oh, probably nothing. I thought I caught a glimpse of something strange off in the mist there. Must have been the light from above playing optical tricks."

"Doctor Love, Doctor Love," sounded the metallic voice of the colonel. "Is everything okay with you? Over."

"Yes, Colonel," answered the girl biologist. "No bogey men have grabbed us yet. We're still dropping down. Can't see a darn thing and we're relying on our radar to avoid hitting the sides."

"Good thing you didn't tell him you were relying on me," said Gabe. "It would really scare him."

"The steam is spewing up all around us," said Jan to the distant Colonel Weeks. "The whole experience so far is something like riding an elevator through a sauna bath. We've now descended to about——"

"Eight thousand feet," supplied Gabe.

"Eight thousand feet," Jan told the colonel. "Which means we're now somewhat lower than the floor level of the jungle outside."

Gabe said, "Instruments indicate we're within one hundred feet of the bottom."

"We're nearly at the bottom of the volcano, Colonel."

Behind the girl, Karl said, "Jan, look, over there. I'm not wrong about it this time."

"Something big is moving toward our copter," Jan told the radio. "Just below us, moving fast. Good gosh, I can see it now! Why, it's a giant b——!"

Colonel Weeks was leaning close to the radio speaker in the Jungle Patrol radio room.

From out of the radio came an enormous, rending, smashing sound. Then there was an angry metallic sputtering, followed by dead silence.

"Doctor Love, Doctor Love! What's happened? Over."

Only silence answered him.

CHAPTER FIVE

Colonel Weeks's big hand clutched the shoulder of the Jungle Patrol radioman. "Keep trying," he said.

Five long minutes had passed since Doctor Jan Love's voice had abruptly ceased coming to them. Outside the afternoon was waning, the heat of the day diminishing.

"Doctor Love, Jungle Patrol calling," said the freckled young radio operator. "Jungle Patrol calling Doctor Love. Come in, please."

Only more silence.

"No contact, sir. Their radio's dead."

The gray-haired colonel winced slightly at that last word. Then nodding his head, he moved to a phone. "Sergeant Barnum?" he said when his aid answered.

"Yes, sir," replied Barnum. "I was about to drop over there to the radio shack and find out how Doc Love is doing. Have you——?"

"I want a Patrol copter sent out to the Veiled Lady at once," ordered Colonel Weeks. "Alert Sandy and Smythe at our Llongo-country base. I want them to fly over that volcano."

"Sir," said the sergeant, "is there something wrong?"

"That's what I'm hoping Sandy and Smythe can find out," replied the commander. "Their orders are to fly over and observe. Under no circumstances are they to go into the volcano."

"Did Doc Love crash or what?"

"At this point we don't know, Sergeant."

36

"Could it have anything to do with Gabe McClennan?" asked Sergeant Barnum. "I just found out something funny from Corporal Gillis."

The colonel had his eyes on the radio, but he turned back to the phone as he asked, "What did he say?"

"Well, about a year or so ago there was a traffic tieup out near where Fred Orlando, that other copter pilot, lives," said Barnum. "And his wife called us to rush a JP ambulance through the jam and take Orlando to the hospital. Corporal Gillis was in charge of the detail. Seems a milk wagon tipped over on the——"

"What was wrong with Orlando?"

"Appendicitis," answered Sergeant Barnum.

"Damn it!" said the colonel, bringing one fist slamming down. "So either he or Gabe was lying this morning. If only I'd known in time to ask him about it over the radio!"

"Can't you ask now?"

"I wish I could." The colonel hung up, and crossed the room to stand behind the radioman. "Anything?"

"Absolutely nothing, sir."

"Well, keep trying," said the colonel. "They may simply have had some minor problem with their radio."

"Didn't sound like that, sir. The way that girl shouted sounded to me like——"

"Keep trying," repeated Colonel Weeks. He began a nervous pacing. "What did she run into? 'Why, it's a gigantic b——!' was the last thing she said. Damn, what did that b stand for?"

"Bird?" suggested the radioman. "Or maybe bull, if they were near the ground."

"Not something that starts with a b," said the colo-

37

nel with a snort. "Something that starts with a b sound. Like . . . beast, behemoth. . . ."

The radioman shrugged. "I give up."

"Well, I'll be in my office," said Colonel Weeks. "Let me know as soon as you make contact."

"Yes, sir," said the freckled young man. "Jungle Patrol calling Doctor Love . . . Jungle Patrol calling Doctor Love. . . ."

The commander walked out into the dying day.

Far from the Jungle Patrol headquarters and the port city of Mawitaan lie the Deep Woods. Modern civilization has been unable, or perhaps unwilling, to penetrate the Deep Woods and so it remains an untamed and mysterious place, filled with wild, strange, and secret things.

In the heart of the Deep Woods is a great cave gnawed into a high, gray cliffside. The jagged mouth of the cave looks, to the relatively few who have seen it, like nothing so much as an enormous skull. . . .

As the day ended, other ears listened to the anxious voice of the young radio operator.

"Doctor Love, come in please . . . Jungle Patrol calling. Over."

The young voice echoed inside the shadowy Skull Cave, bouncing from the cave walls.

To one side of the vast cave a dais rose and atop this dais was a stone throne. The skull motif was repeated here; a grinning skeleton head had been roughly carved out of the stone.

Sitting casually on this formidable throne was a broad-shouldered, magnificently muscled man who seemed to be no older than thirty. He was masked and wore a skintight costume with a death's head grinning from the buckle of his gunbelt. The fingers of his powerful right hand were steepled on his crossed knee. As he listened he raised the fingers from his knee and moved them to pat one of the holsters at his side.

Stretched out at the masked man's feet was a handsome animal that resembled a German Shepherd. Actually, it was a mountain wolf. When the man touched his holster, the animal pricked his ears, looking up at his master's face.

Standing up, the masked man left the dais and moved closer to the powerful radio set which kept him in contact with Jungle Patrol headquarters. The big wolf rose to follow him, making a gentle rumbling sound in its chest.

"I don't think it's any use," said the far-away radio operator to himself. "No use at all."

The masked man turned toward the mouth of the great cave. "What do you think, Guran?"

Squatting just inside the cave was a tiny gray-brown man. He was chunky and hardly more than three feet high. He wore a hemp skirt and a broad hat made of thatch. Resting close at hand was a short, poison-tipped spear. Guran was a member of the Bandar pygmy tribe, the little people who were the only ones who dared to dwell in the Deep Woods. Still hunkered on the threshold, Guran replied, "I think once again the old stories have been proven true, Phantom."

The Phantom left the radio, and walked over to his old friend. "You mean the stories about the deadliness of the Veiled Lady?"

"Yes, Phantom," answered the pygmy. "It is said, and I believe truly said, that no one of the jungle has ever entered that volcano and returned to tell the tale." Guran shook his head, giving a small shudder. "It is a place of death—a place of sacrifice."

"Not of sacrifice any longer, Guran," reminded the Phantom. "That was all centuries ago, wasn't it?"

'Yes, many centuries ago," answered the pygmy. "In the days when the first Phantom walked the jungle." The Bandar people had lived in this mysterious wood for centuries, even before the coming of the first Phantom. Guran had known the present Phantom since he was a child.

The Phantom began to pace the stone floor of the Skull Cave, with the wolf, Devil, at his heels. "I wonder what that girl and her party ran into down there," he mused. "What was it she said? 'It's a gigantic b——!' What does that b stand for? And what did she find within the Veiled Lady?"

"Death," Guran told him. "That is what waits for everyone who tries to learn the secrets of the Veiled Lady."

With a smile, the Phantom said, "And you think that would happen to me, too? Guran, should I give it a try?"

The pygmy jumped to his feet, clutching his spear. "You're not thinking of going to look for that foolish female doctor, are you, Phantom?"

"I'll wait and see what Colonel Weeks's patrol helicopter finds out," the Phantom said. Though none knew it, the Phantom himself was actually commander in chief of the Jungle Patrol. Even Colonel Weeks did not know the identity of the mysterious commander in chief from whom his orders came, though the shrewd colonel had a strong suspicion. "I have a hunch they aren't going to learn anything by flying over the Veiled Lady."

Guran stood with his spear held at the ready in

front of him, as though he were about to be attacked by something. "I have a hunch, a premonition, too, Phantom."

"Which is?"

"It is that you will face great danger should you seek to find that girl," said Guran. "Well . . . perhaps you will not have to go at all. Yes, perhaps." He turned from the Phantom, making his way out into the twilight.

CHAPTER SIX

Sergeant Barnum pushed the wooden door of the radio room open with one big, booted foot and stepped in out of the night. The darkness behind him was filled with the restless hum of insects and night birds. "I brought you something from the commissary," announced the stocky sergeant, tipping his chin in the direction of the tray he was carrying.

The colonel sat in the shadows, his gray head bent, his blunt fingers pressing against his cheeks. "What?" he asked, looking up.

There was a new man on the radio now. He made a hopeless shrug in the direction of the approaching sergeant.

Brushing aside a pile of papers, Sergeant Barnum set the dinner tray atop a desk near the commander. "I brought you some dinner, sir."

"Anything new from Sandy and Smythe?" asked Colonel Weeks.

"They've returned to base," answered the sergeant. "You ordered them not to descend into the Veiled Lady."

"No, there's no use losing them, too."

"You don't know Doctor Love is lost," Sergeant Barnum pointed out while he took the silver covers off the various serving dishes. "All you know for sure is that her radio is on the blink. Maybe all the steam in the volcano caused that. I know on humid days I have a heck of a time bringing in the opera broadcasts on. . . ."

"I should never have allowed her to go," said Colonel Weeks. His pipe had long since gone dead. He tapped it absently on his knee. "A vulnerable young girl like her."

"Doctor Love handled herself pretty well around here," the sergeant reminded him.

"The pistol range, the gymnasium. Those are simple everyday challenges compared to—compared to lord knows what she ran into down there. What did she mean when she said, 'It's a gigantic b——!'?" He rose out of the shadows, strode toward a tape recorder on a work bench.

"Fasting isn't going to help you solve the problem any quicker, sir." Sergeant Barnum nodded at the tray of steaming food. "As a matter of fact, I read someplace that protein helps the brain to——"

"Be quiet, Sergeant, I want to play this tape again," said the gray-haired Jungle Patrol commander.

The sergeant picked up a mug of coffee from the tray. "At least, drink this."

The colonel frowned, then took the tan mug and sipped at the hot coffee. He jabbed the playback button on the tape machine and listened, for the tenth time, to the last message from Doctor Jan Love.

Her frightened voice repeated once again, "Just below us, moving fast. Good gosh, I can see it now. Why, it's a giant b——!"

As the girl's voice faded away, Colonel Weeks said, "What could it have been?" He sat hunched forward, his lips forming the letter b over and over, trying to guess what came next.

Large glistening red ants were marching across the rough wooden floor of another radio shack. This one was far to the South of Mawitaan, in a rundown scatter of outpost buildings on the route to the Llongo country. The light of the hanging oil lamp made the hurrying scarlet ants glow as though they were on fire.

Tinn, the weary-looking Chinese, did a little hopping dance as he crossed the room, avoiding the lines of red ants and the other skittering insects. He studied a lopsided wooden chair, poking at a black spot on the seat. The spot scurried away. Sighing, Tinn sat down. He began to construct himself a new cigarette. "Anything new?" he asked.

Sitting before the radio set was a small dark man in a soiled checkered shirt and ancient khaki trousers. He was about forty years old, with bright, deep-set eyes. "Not a single damn word," said Silvera. He glanced at his bare elbow, then slapped at the flying insect that had alighted there. "One would think that smudge you exhale would keep all these rascals at a distance."

Tinn blew out smoke, watching Silvera. "We'd better get in touch with Barber."

"I'm not anxious," said Silvera. "One likes to avoid those harangues of his."

"The longer we wait, the longer the harangue," said Tinn, puffing on his homemade cigarette. "He's going to blame us for all this, no matter what we say."

Silvera pointed a lean finger at the radio set. "It's not my fault that damn Gabe hasn't seen fit to communicate with us."

Eyes half-closed, Tinn asked, "You think he's dead?"

Silvera shrugged. "It's possible. One hesitates to pronounce him dead on insufficient evidence."

"But you heard Doctor Love go off the air, you told

me," said the Chinese. "That was before I arrived at this hole. She stopped dead in mid-broadcast, didn't she?"

"She did indeed," said Silvera. "Gave one goose-bumps, the frightened scream she gave out."

"Okay, suppose they crashed and are all dead. It's no use our sitting around here, letting the bugs feast on us."

Nodding slowly, Silvera said, "Very well. We will beard the lion and report to the chief." The dark little man fiddled with the radio set for a few moments.

"Finally," spoke Barber back in his office at the Scarlet Cockatoo. "What does Gabe report from inside?"

Silvera backed away from the radio speaker, as though it were the pale fat Barber in person. "Nothing, not a single damn word."

"What? Do you mean you've been unable to make contact with him?"

"I don't mean that at all. On the contrary, it is Gabe who hasn't gotten in touch with us."

"Why?"

"There's a possibility he's dead."

"Dead? What happened to them?"

"One can only guess," said Silvera. He told the distant Barber about the last message from Doctor Love which he'd monitored.

Barber cleared his throat, an angry rumbling sound. "I was certain she knew what she was doing," he said. "Though it's possible this is . . . yes, it's possible this is only a coverup. She may be feigning silence so she can go after the treasure in secret."

"I didn't get the impression the girl was putting on an act."

"I'm not interested in your subjective judgments,

Silvera. I'm interested only in the fortune I know the Veiled Lady holds," replied Barber's voice. "I'm convinced Doctor Love has knowledge of that wealth. Well, then—you'll have to find out."

"Find out what?"

"Find out what's going on down there in the volcano."

"But if Gabe doesn't contact us, how can we?"

"You'll have to take alternative measures," suggested Barber.

"Such as?"

"Perhaps you'll have to find a way to get down inside the Veiled Lady yourselves," Barber told him.

CHAPTER SEVEN

Dawn was coming to the Deep Woods, the night chill was fading, and a soft pink light began to fill the jungle. Awakening birds commenced their chirping; hungry cubs growled.

Near the massive Skull Cave, the tiny pygmy warrior Guran stirred, then sat upright and wide awake. "You rise early today, Phantom," he said. His grip on his poison-tipped spear relaxed as he realized it was the sounds made by the masked man that had awakened him.

The Phantom was tightening the cinch on the saddle of his white stallion, Hero. "It's a long ride to the Llongo country," he told his long-time friend. "I want to get an early start, Guran."

The pygmy rubbed a small hand over the tufted top of his head. He put on his wide thatch hat, adjusting it with a pull. "So you've decided to pay her a visit?"

"The Veiled Lady, yes."

Brush and wispy ferns far to their right began to sway and both men turned to look. It was Devil, returning from his morning romp.

The big gray wolf trotted up to watch his master, panting happily in anticipation of a new adventure.

Guran lifted his hat to scratch his head once more. "I could warn you again not to go near the Veiled Lady," he said. "But I know it would do no good. When you have made up your mind, nothing can stop you."

The Phantom grinned at the little gray-brown man. "I respect your advice, Guran," he said. "However, I want to find out what happened to the girl and her party. As you know, the Jungle Patrol copter brought back no new information after flying over the volcano. Colonel Weeks has heard nothing more from Doctor Love since that interrupted message yesterday afternoon. I'm going to the Veiled Lady. If there's a chance. . . ."

"Yes, I know. If there's a chance, no matter how slim, that those foolish scientists can be rescued, the Phantom will take it." The pygmy's serious expression was spoiled by a chuckle. "Oh, yes, I know."

The Phantom swung lightly up into the saddle. "The Llongo tribe live near the volcano," he said. "I want you to send word to their chief. Tell him I'd like him to meet me at the head of the River of Fire."

Guran nodded. "It will be done," he told the masked man. "No need to wish you luck, since I know the Phantom makes his own. Good-bye."

"I'll see you again soon," the Phantom assured the little man. He made a gentle clucking sound and the great stallion galloped away along the jungle trail which led away from the Skull Cave.

Giving a pleased growl, Devil started running in their wake.

Soon, as the Phantom sped through the tangle of the Deep Woods, the sound of pygmy drums was heard. His message to the chief of the Llongo tribe was on its way.

The chief of the peaceful Llongo tribe was a large plump man in his middle years. He wore a headdress of scarlet plumes and polished bones interwoven with gold. His cloak was of a similar shade of scarlet,

48

trimmed with white plumes. Now in the mid-afternoon, he was moving with his entourage of warriors toward the great volcano.

The trees and foliage bordering the path toward the Veiled Lady were damp and a fine mist drifted perpetually through the branches and among the thick, hanging leaves.

The chief paused once again, mopping at his broad brow with one plump hand. "I would not undertake such a trip for everyone," he confided to the large black warrior at his side. "For the Phantom of course. . . ." He trailed off into a panting sigh, resuming his stride.

The mist grew thicker as they neared the base of the veiled volcano. They could hear a loud gushing roar. It was here that the hot river known as the River of Fire had its origin. It came rushing out of the mountainside about a hundred feet up, a waterfall of heated water, and then began its rush down through the Llongo country, through forests and through rolling fields where the Llongo herds grazed. The water spit out tangles of steam and warm spray as it fell down the cliffside to splash on the volcanic rocks at the commencement of the river's course.

The chief halted two dozen yards from the hot river, raising a hand. His party stopped behind him. Wiping his brow again, the chief squinted at the Veiled Lady. The mountain rose up and was lost in the mist at its distant peak. "I do not like this place," he said finally. "Were it not for the Phantom I would never——"

"He comes," whispered a warrior.

From out of the mist to their left stepped the tall broad-shouldered masked man. He was leading his stallion, his right hand was held high in greeting.

"Phantom," said the chief, beaming. "Oh, Ghost Who Walks, welcome. Welcome, oh, Man Who Cannot Die."

"I am honored," said the Phantom when he halted near the Llongo chief and his party. "Honored that you, great and wise ruler of the peaceful and industrious Llongo people, have come here to greet me, along with your bravest warriors."

After a few more similar courtesies were exchanged, the plump chief drew the Phantom to one side. "There is trouble, Ghost Who Walks? We have heard the Jungle Patrol plane buzzing high above us. And we have heard that someone has fallen into the very mouth of the volcano."

"That's true," replied the masked man. "Yesterday two scientists and their pilot made an attempt to fly down into the Veiled Lady in a helicopter."

"Ah, I see."

"Did your people notice anything yesterday?"

"No, nothing save the Jungle Patrol ship."

"You know nothing about what might have happened to those people?"

"Alas, no, Ghost Who Walks." The chief shook his head, causing the scarlet plumes to flutter. "I would guess they are dead now, like all the others. No one has ever returned alive from the Veiled Lady." He pointed skyward.

Not following the gesture, the Phantom kept his gaze on the chief. "What do you mean, Chief, about others?"

The chief laid a plump hand on the Phantom's brawny arm. "Look up that way," he said, pointing again. "You can barely make it out if you strain your eyes. Way up there at the very lip of the volcano is a

50

flattened-out area known as the bare spot. Evil things were done there in days long past."

"I know of the sacrifices," said the Phantom.

The Llongo chieftain said, "In ancient days, maidens were hurled alive from that bare spot as a sacrifice to the angry gods. Not only maidens, but much gold and precious stones and carvings of ivory, so we are told." He gave a sad shake of his head. "We have thought it best to let whatever treasure there is rest down there forever. Even if a man could climb down and survive to find the treasure, he would never be able to return alive."

The Phantom did not reply. He turned his back on the mountain to study the down-rushing steaming River of Fire.

The chief's eyes looked that way, too. "Our old legends tell us this river is made of the hot tears of the Veiled Lady," he continued. "Tears of pity shed for the poor young girls who were so cruelly sacrificed."

"Wait now." The Phantom suddenly sprinted to the river's edge. He snatched up a stick to poke at something spinning in the rumbling waters. "That flower, it comes from inside the volcano."

The plump chief slowly moved to join the masked man. "Such flowers grow nowhere else on earth, I believe," he explained as the Phantom rescued the gigantic bloom from the River of Fire. "It is from the heart of the Veiled Lady."

The flower was white and crimson, many-petaled. It was shaped like a giant cup, like an intricately worked grail, and measured fully twelve inches across. The Phantom held the dripping blossom in the palms of both hands. "If this flower grew in there, then there is life at the bottom of the volcano."

All at once a realization came to the chief. He gave

a loud exclamation, took a step backward. "I have not yet asked you the reason for your visit," he said. "Surely you don't intend to——?"

"Yes," the Phantom said to him. "I'm going to visit the Veiled Lady."

CHAPTER EIGHT

Alone now, the Phantom began his long climb. Slung over one broad shoulder was a long, coiled rope, which the Llongo people had helped him make from sturdy vines. The priests of centuries before had caused a rough stairway to be carved into the mountainside. The Phantom was following this on his ascent toward the sacrificial bare spot.

Hearing weapons and ornaments jangle far below, he looked down. The plump Llongo chief waved a final farewell before he and his entourage turned away. The chief's shoulders had a sad slouch. He was certain that not even the Phantom could survive a visit to the Veiled Lady.

The Phantom, before starting his upward journey, had entrusted his stallion Hero and the wolf Devil to the care of the Llongo chief. Sensing his master was gazing down at him, the big wolf gave a mournful howl, protesting their separation.

The retreating Llongos blurred. Soon the swirling mist put a wall of white between the masked man and everyone and everything on the ground. He was wrapped in solitude, alone with the towering mountain.

He maintained a steady pace, working ever higher. Silence seemed to flow all around him with the mist.

Eventually, the Phantom reached the place of ancient sacrifice, the bare spot. Standing with hands on hips, he surveyed the chasm into which he must go.

"Can't see the bottom at all," the masked man said to himself.

Spiraling up toward him were great billows of steamy mist.

Kneeling on one knee, the Phantom scanned the volcano interior immediately below him. The wall looks to be sheer for a good hundred feet or more, he thought. But then she starts a gradual slope. I'll try to reach that slope, then see what comes next.

Nearby in the mist, something scraped rock.

The masked man rose, spun, his hand dropping toward a holster. Then he relaxed, grinning. "Have you come to give me a going-away party?"

Climbing up out of the fog was little Guran, and behind him came a half-dozen Bandar, the pygmy people. "I decided to journey out of the Deep Woods," said Guran.

"So I see. But why?"

"To make one more attempt to persuade you not to enter this evil mountain," said the Phantom's old friend. With a spear he gestured at the spirals of mist beyond the rim. "This is an accursed place, Phantom. A place of death."

The masked man stepped forward, placing a hand on the pygmy's shoulder. "I must go, Guran," he told him. "The girl and her friends may still be alive down there."

Guran watched the Phantom's face for a few seconds. "Very well then," he said at last. With both hands, he held out the spear he'd been carrying. "I would like you to take this spear with you, Phantom. It is specially prepared against evil."

The Phantom knew this meant the spear was tipped with an extra-strong dose of poison. He felt his guns would serve him better against anything he might encounter below, but he accepted his long-time friend's gesture. "Thank you, Guran. I will carry it with me."

"That pleases me, Phantom," said Guran as he handed over the weapon.

The masked man swung the spear over his shoulder, and sheathed it in the back of his wide gunbelt. "I've left Hero and Devil with the Llongos," said the Phantom. He unslung the coil of vine rope, began playing it out. "Will you wait with the Llongo people until I return?"

The gray-brown pygmy caught up the end of the rope and set about securing it to a rock. "We will return to the Deep Woods."

"Very well." The Phantom waited until the rope was fastened, then gave it a hard, testing tug. "I'll see you back at the Skull Cave."

Guran said, "Yes, back at the cave." He stood quietly, watching.

Nodding at him, with a grin, the Phantom backed over the edge of the bare spot. He went over and began working his way, wide-legged, down the sheer vertical wall of the ancient volcano.

Guran squatted at the lip of the flat sacrifice stone. After a few moments the lithe figure of the Phantom sank down out of sight, swallowed by the thick, spinning mist. The little man remained staring down for several minutes more. At last, he stood and told the other pygmies, "We will go now."

"When will we see him again?" asked one of the others.

"Soon," replied Guran.

A large dry leaf, shaped like the spade on an ace of spades, fell down to jiggle Tinn's hand. Grains of gold-brown tobacco spilled out of his cigarette paper, splashing flecks on his boots. The weary-looking Chinese was slouched against the bole of a wide-trunked gnarled tree. "What's happening now?" he asked casually.

Up above him, stretched out on the broad twisting arms of the high forest tree, was Silvera. He had a pair of dented binoculars pressed to his eyes and was watching the Veiled Lady, which loomed a quarter of a mile in the distance. "He went right over the edge, I think," said Silvera. "One can't be all that sure with so much fog blowing about up there."

"But you're certain it's the Phantom?"

"Well, how many masked men are there in this damned jungle? Of course it's the Phantom."

Another large leaf came plummeting down and Tinn swung his nearly completed cigarette out of the way. "We ought to go home, back to Mawitaan."

"Oh, yes—Barber, he'd like that. One can envision the scene when you and I appear, looking a little sheepish, to tell him the Phantom frightened us away."

"The Phantom does frighten me," said Tinn. "That's the truth."

"Here come those little pygmy rascals," said Silvera up in the tree. "They're making their way back down the volcano side. That's good."

"What's good about it?"

"One assumes thereby that the Phantom is going down into the Veiled Lady all by himself." Silvera shifted his position slightly. "We won't have to worry about running into a pack of poison-throwing little savages as well."

Tinn lit his new cigarette. "No, all we have to worry about is the Phantom," he said. "And whatever it was that probably killed Gabe."

"One has to consider the odds." Silvera lifted the glasses to rub at his eyes. "Two of us against the Phantom is better odds than two of us against him and a whole troop of pygmy savages."

"I suppose," said Tinn, puffing.

Silvera frowned down at the tired Chinese. "I'll tell you something, Tinn. The reason Barber sits comfortably back in Mawitaan while you work your tail off out in the jungle is because of your negative attitude toward life. I sense a distinct air of defeatism about you."

Exhaling smoke, Tinn asked, "And how come you're up in a tree in the same jungle with me?"

"Circumstances," answered Silvera. "Circumstances have forced me to work far below my true capacities." He returned the binoculars to the case hanging around his neck. "Now we have to wait until the horde of savages clear out."

"You really think it's possible to get down into the Veiled Lady?"

"The Phantom went, didn't he?" Silvera nimbly swung down through the interlacing of wide branches. Hitting the ground, he added, "I've been doing some research, talking to people who know this Llongo country. Now, one assumes our masked friend just availed himself of the place I've been told about. It's called the bare spot."

"That's where they tossed the girls over."

"Not only girls, Tinn, but treasure," said Silvera. "Imagine throwing away money and women."

"Imagine falling straight down ten thousand feet."

Silvera shook his head. "I think there's a good bit of superstitious nonsense connected with this mountain," he said. "The actual descent may not be all that difficult."

Tinn took a long puff. "You're determined to give it a try?"

"I'm not saying we'll have to climb," Silvera told him. "There may be an easier, much easier way. I'm going to try to persuade our fat friend to pay for it."

"What easier way?" asked the weary-looking Chinese. "You don't mean flying, going in by copter?"

"And why not? I'm a fully accredited pilot . . . well, not accredited in this particular backward country, but a damn good flyer nevertheless."

"So was Gabe."

"We'll succeed where he failed," said the little dark man.

"So you say." Tinn threw his cigarette away into the brush.

CHAPTER NINE

Letting go of his vine rope, the Phantom dropped five feet to a rocky ledge, scattering pebbles when he landed. Here the sheer cliff ended and the gradual slope began. Taking out Guran's spear, the masked man held it like a staff as he looked down.

It was warmer here, the mist more steamy. The Phantom started down the slope of the Veiled Lady's interior.

After a moment he nearly stumbled, for something snapped underfoot. Bending, the Phantom said, "So there were indeed sacrifices here in olden days."

Sprawled near the rim of the ledge was the broken skeleton of a young girl. It was centuries' old. There were no other skeletons around, only this one lying alone.

"The others must have fallen further below," observed the masked man. "This poor girl landed here by accident." Stepping around the bones, he resumed his downward way.

He was able to progress on foot now, but he had to move slowly and carefully. The mist was so thick he could never be certain what awaited him a few feet further down. Waves of fog lapped at him.

The Phantom took one more careful step and suddenly the rock surface he had touched snapped and cracked away beneath his booted foot.

The slippery slope side hit hard against his side as he fell and went sliding down. Rough rocks hit at him like fists as he rolled and tumbled. The masked man grabbed out for something to hold on to, something to halt his fall. Everything he clutched at was slippery and elusive.

Finally, pushing out with his powerful legs and throwing himself sideways, the Phantom got hold of an outcropping of rock. He held tight to it, regaining his balance.

Now, poking with his spear end as if it were a blind man's stick, he continued his downward journey. It seemed to grow a little—only a little—easier. Occasionally, as he made his difficult descent, the Phantom paused to scratch a mark on an outcropping of rock with his Skull Ring. If he had to return this way he wanted to be able to find his course again.

Surefooted and careful, the Phantom continued down the rocky incline, descending, gradually, thousands of feet down.

It was hot as the hottest day of summer now. The mist was thinning as he reached ground level.

Suddenly, up overhead, came a giant whirring sound. Instinctively the Phantom ducked, while thrusting upward with his spear.

The loud droning faded away in the mist.

What was that? the Phantom thought. He'd gotten no clear look at what it was which had zoomed through the fog. A flying boulder, or maybe a flying truck from the sound of it.

Soon he felt moss and thick grass beneath his boots. "Last stop, everybody out," said the Phantom.

The air was relatively clear here. The masked man found himself in a vast tropical forest. Spotted here and there among the thick, lush foliage were geysers which spouted up steam.

"When that steam hits the cooler air up above it makes the mist," he said. "So this is the secret of the lady's veils."

Far to his right he noticed more skeletons, a great mound of bleached bones—all that was left of the maidens who had been sacrificed to the long-dead gods. The Phantom's head bowed for an instant before he continued on.

Spear in hand, he strode across the soft moss. "I wonder where their copter came down," he mused.

The Phantom halted, cupped a hand to his mouth, and shouted, "Hallo, Doctor Love! Hallo, can you hear me? Doctor Love!"

No answer came.

The masked man called out once more and then resumed his trek into this valley which lay in the heart of the Veiled Lady.

Half an hour later the Phantom stopped once again to call. "Doctor Love! Hallo, Doctor Love!"

Still no one answered his hail.

The masked man was frowning, studying the foliage through which he had been moving. He went over to a large stalk which rose up to a height of ten feet. "This is very familiar-looking, but I can't quite place it."

Near the base of the stalk lay an enormous splash of white, the size of an unfurled pennant. Kneeling, the Phantom touched it. Hey, it's a flower petal, a gigantic flower petal, he thought. Snapping his fingers, he said aloud, "And this thing here is a wild flower— but a wild flower ten feet tall."

He stood, scanning the surrounding area. "There— that's an orchid plant, with orchids the size of a man or bigger. And those ferns over there must reach to a height of thirty feet!"

The Phantom heard something in the brush. He turned. "Look at that fellow," he said.

Making his way along the mossy ground, carrying a twig the size of a baseball bat, was an ant. This ant was as large as a house cat. Seeing his three-section body, his waving antennae, his half-dozen legs so clearly made you feel as though you were studying him under a powerful microscope.

But this is no optical illusion, the Phantom thought as he blinked and shook his head. This is real. What kind of place is this?

The leaves of the giant flower rustled.

Looking up, the Phantom exclaimed, "Whew!"

Flapping above him was a beautiful yellow-and-purple butterfly. Its wing spread was a full twelve feet.

I feel as though, thought the Phantom, I were Jack in that beanstalk fairy tale. This is like some giant's hothouse.

He watched the enormous butterfly flap up to lose itself in the high mist.

The Phantom continued to explore the volcanic valley. Everything he encountered was a giant version of something in the world outside the Veiled Lady. Plants which were tiny in the Deep Woods stretched up tall as trees here. Weeds grew higher than men, with seedpods the size of ripe pumpkins. The insects were of animal size. Red and black ants roamed the valley, looking like packs of dogs in size.

"I wonder if Doctor Love expected any of this," said the Phantom.

Up ahead of him he saw a great green grasshopper, with one of its legs resting on something black. When the big insect sensed him its membranous wings opened and it gave a flying hop up and away, looking like a large model airplane on the loose.

The Phantom picked up the black object. It was a notebook, with a pebbled leather cover. Each page was filled with notations in neat, tiny printing. This must be Doctor Love's, concluded the Phantom, tucking the book into his belt.

Off among the foliage to his right, he sensed a large dark shape huddling. The Phantom planted his booted feet wide, turned with ready spear.

It was the helicopter.

The ship looked like a broken toy among the giant plants and flowers.

"Doctor Love," called the Phantom. "Doctor Love, are you here?"

No response came.

The copter's rotor blades were bent like the fingers of an old man's hand. The flying machine was tilted far to one side.

Slowly, the Phantom worked his way through the tangle of overgrown plant life.

He took a deep breath and held it when he came near the cockpit. Exhaling, he said, "No one inside at all."

The cracked cabin glass was zigzagged with fine lines. His face pressed to it, the Phantom studied the inside of the crashed helicopter. Radio's smashed, he noted to himself. Which explains why she couldn't contact Colonel Weeks to ask for help.

He stepped back from the downed ship and began studying the ground all around the crash site.

"What's this?" he asked aloud. He bent, touching the ground with his fingertips. A splotch of red stained the moss. "Blood. So at least one of the three is hurt."

The Phantom found a second scarlet dot, then a

third. "Traces of footprints, too. Looks like they headed off in this——"

Above him a great buzzing was growing.

Straightening, the Phantom turned to face the approaching source of the ominous sound.

CHAPTER TEN

Colonel Weeks came striding across the gravel parking lot behind Jungle Patrol headquarters. Taking his place in the jeep, he gave Sergeant Barnum an address, adding, "He's supposed to be home today, according to the people at the field."

The stocky sergeant put the machine in gear and they roared away. "You think this might have something to do with Doctor Love's crash?" he asked.

Lines showed on the commander's forehead. "We don't know there's been a crash, Sergeant," he reminded his aide. "All we know is she hasn't communicated with us since yesterday."

Sergeant Barnum concentrated on his driving for a while, taking the jeep through the narrow dusty streets and alleyways of Mawitaan, cutting sharply round corners and easing through the thick afternoon traffic on the wide thoroughfares of the market area. European and American cars mingled with horse-drawn carts; messengers on motor scooters cut around native women with wicker baskets balanced on their heads.

When the jeep was climbing uphill away from the sea, the sergeant asked, "You think Gabe McClennan had something to do with . . . with whatever happened?"

The gray-haired colonel bit on the stem of his pipe for a few long seconds. Faint smudges of shadow under his eyes indicated he hadn't slept much since the disappearance of Doctor Love and her party. "I like to build cases on facts," he said finally.

"Hey!" Sergeant Barnum hit the brake, in time to avoid hitting a stray piebald goat which was clacking its way across the narrow cobblestone street.

When the jeep started up again, Colonel Weeks continued, "Right now we don't have anything against Gabe. Nothing except his past record, and I don't like to hound a man because of that. The thing is, Sergeant, I can't keep from wondering why Orlando didn't take the helicopter into the Veiled Lady. He was the pilot originally scheduled for the job."

"Okay, suppose he wasn't sick," said the sergeant. "Maybe he got hoodooed. Everybody's heard stories about the volcano. Orlando's a family man and all."

"That's occurred to me," admitted the colonel. "I can't help it, though, Sergeant, I've got a hunch— a hunch that something is not quite right."

"Here's the house." Sergeant Barnum parked the jeep against the curb.

They were in a block of fresh, white two-story homes. The stucco, tile-roofed houses were so close together they gave the impression they were all segments of a block-long wall.

After the colonel rang the bell, an iron grille in the heavy wooden door swung open and a little hand appeared where a face was supposed to look out. A tiny voice asked, "Yes, what is it please?"

"Is your father home?" Sergeant Barnum said.

"I think he's sick," answered the tiny child's voice. "I don't think he can see anybody."

"Tell him the Jungle Patrol wants to talk with him," said the sergeant. "It's very important."

"Okay, I'll tell him."

The colonel touched Barnum's arm. "There's a side

entrance off the alley between houses. Go watch it."

"You think he'll try a skip?"

"Another hunch."

The sergeant nodded, trotting off.

A kitten's fuzzy face appeared at the peephole in the door. "This is my new cat," announced the tiny voice. "I'm holding him up so you can see her."

"Very handsome," said Colonel Weeks. "Now I'd like to see your father."

"He's too sick," explained the unseen child in the Orlando home.

"Hey! Hold it!" came Sergeant Barnum's voice from the narrow passageway between the bright white houses.

"I haven't got a name for him yet, but——"

The colonel pivoted on one foot, running to join the sergeant.

He found the stocky Barnum grappling with a middle-sized dark young man against the iron-grille fence at the alley's end.

"He runs pretty good for a guy with his appendix just out," remarked the sergeant.

"All right, Orlando," said Colonel Weeks to the pilot. "What's this all about?"

"My doctor says I'm not supposed to have visitors."

"Your doctor also says you had your appendix out over a year ago," the colonel reminded him. He put one big weathered hand on the pilot's shoulder. "Why are you pretending to be sick?"

Orlando straightened, and ran his fingers through his curly hair. "Oh, I got scared," he said, trying a smile on the colonel and then the sergeant. "When you're a family man you can't, you know, afford to take too many daredevil jobs."

Colonel Weeks had his big hand still pressing the

young man's shoulder. "I don't think you'd dodge us simply because you didn't want to admit to being a coward," he said. "Now you listen to me, Orlando. Right now three people are missing, one of them a woman. I want to know what happened to those three and I'm going to keep at it until I do." He swung his other hand up to clutch the pilot's other shoulder. "This may even turn out to be murder, Orlando."

"Gabe wasn't going to kill anybody," said Orlando, trying to back away. He was already up against the black-iron bars of the fence.

"What was he going to do?" demanded the colonel in an even voice.

Orlando kept his eyes from meeting those of the JP commander. "I don't know."

"What did he tell you? Why did he want to take Doctor Love's flight into the Veiled Lady?"

"I'm not sure, Colonel, believe me."

"But Gabe did arrange for you to drop out."

Orlando licked his upper lip before answering. "Not Gabe, exactly."

"Someone else?"

"Look," began Orlando, "I'll tell you what I know, Colonel, but you have to believe me when I say I had no idea Gabe was planning any violence."

"Did they pay you to give him your place?"

Slowly, Orlando nodded. "Yes, two hundred dollars. With a family, you know, that——"

"Who gave you the money?"

"Well, I'm not sure who he was," said Orlando. "A big guy, Portuguese, I think, has a left eye that's always half-closed. He hangs out around the field now and then. I think he might be tied in with one of the shipping companies down by the harbor."

"Lemos," said Sergeant Barnum, recognizing the

man from the description. "That sounds like that guy Lemos."

"Yes, it could be," agreed the colonel. "Now, Orlando, why did he pay you to quit the flight?"

"He wanted Gabe to take it," said Orlando. "He knew if I backed out at the last minute Gabe would be the one to pilot Doctor Love and her buddy."

"Why did they want Gabe to do it?"

"I don't know, Colonel. I really don't know."

The colonel studied the pilot's face for nearly a half minute. "Did you talk to Gabe about any of this?"

"No, sir. I never saw Gabe after this guy—Lemos, is it?—after he paid me. I just stayed home, gave the field my sick story," said Orlando. "I never knew, believe me, Gabe was planning to kill them. Is that what he did?"

"We don't know." The colonel let go of him. "But we're going to find out." He turned, leaving the young man slumped back against the twisted black bars.

When they were back in the jeep Sergeant Barnum asked, "Do we look for Lemos?"

"We do," said the colonel. "I want to find out who he's working for."

CHAPTER ELEVEN

Down through the giant leaves and petals droned an enormous bee, heading straight for the Phantom. Its body was larger than that of a horse, its great whirring wings were several feet in length, and they refracted the afternoon light like stained-glass windows. The bee's deadly stinger was the size of a bayonet. The angry buzzing grew louder as the creature flew toward the Phantom.

Beside the wreckage of Doctor Love's fallen helicopter, the masked man braced himself. "This has to be what she saw," he said. "A gigantic bee. Their ship must have been attacked by one as they were coming down." He kept his eyes on the bee, Guran's poison-tipped spear ready in his hands.

The bee dived right for him. The Phantom dodged to one side, thrusting his spear in and out of the bee's abdomen as it zoomed by.

The creature passed over him, banking and climbing. Its giant whirring wings scattered great flecks of pollen as it turned by the oversized flower stalks. The bee's buzzing took on an even angrier tone as it circled to attack again.

The Phantom readjusted his grip on the spear, awaiting the new charge.

The giant bee began a new dive toward him.

A dozen yards away, it began to wobble.

Suddenly it swerved, went jerking upward as though it had been caught by some powerful gust of wind. The creature corkscrewed through the air. All at once it was silent, like a mechanism which has been switched off.

Leaves, flowers, nuggets of golden pollen came falling down in advance of the plummeting bee.

The Phantom dropped his spear to dive beneath the shelter of the wreck.

With an earth-shaking crash the gigantic bee hit the ground a few feet from the crouching masked man.

"Dead," said the Phantom. "Guran's poison worked." He eased out into the open, caught up the spear. "I have a feeling I may have use for this again."

From out of the underbrush, giant ants came marching to swarm over the dead body of the giant bee.

From above, a flock of winged things flew in, alighting on the huge carcass.

"What kind of birds—hey, they're flies," said the Phantom. "Flies as big as swallows. I guess I still haven't adjusted my sense of proportion to fit this place."

He made one more careful circuit of the downed copter, then climbed inside the ship for a final look around.

"More blood here on the pilot's seat," the masked man observed. "Meaning he's probably the one who's hurt." He scanned the interior. "Looks like they took most of their weapons and supplies, which means they came out of the crash alive."

He jumped to the mossy ground, again followed the trail of blood spots. "The question is—are they still alive?"

As he moved by the body of the dead bee, a half dozen of the bird-size flies left their work to buzz round his head.

"Shoo," suggested the Phantom.

He snapped a shoot off a giant flower. The leaf at its tip was twice the size of a man's hand. It made an excellent fly swatter.

Gabe McClennan grinned at them, then caught at his stomach and fell forward onto the ground. "Another woozy spell," he said in a faint voice. "Maybe you'd best leave me by the side of the road."

"That's enough of that kind of talk," said Karl Waagener, easing an arm around the injured pilot's shoulder. "Here, I'll help you up."

"I haven't seen the vultures in this part of the country yet," said Gabe. "But if they match the rest of the flora and fauna they'll probably think of me as just a quick snack." He got to his feet with the bearded biologist's help.

"That gash in your leg is bleeding again, Gabe," noticed Doctor Jan Love, who, armed with a .300 Weatherby Magnum big-game rifle, was bringing up the rear.

Karl scanned the jungle of giant grass and ferns they were trekking through. "Looks like a cave over there, Jan, in that scatter of giant rocks. What say we rest there for a spell?"

"Resting isn't going to get us out of here," said Gabe.

"We can afford to take a break," said Jan. "I'll have another look at your leg and change the dressing."

As he hobbled ahead, holding on to Karl's arm, the pilot said, "Well, okay. I'm sorry to be keeping you folks from your work."

Jan brushed her long blonde hair back from her face. "Are you kidding? We've seen more fantastic specimens in the last twenty-four hours than we'd be likely to see in a lifetime on the outside."

"And they've seen us," added Karl. "I can't get over the odd sensation of having an insect look me in the eye."

Gabe was frowning. "I don't mean all these overgrown bugs," he said. "Aren't you people interested in. . . ." His voice trailed off.

"In what, Gabe?" Karl asked him.

"Never mind," replied Gabe. "I guess I'm babbling. Forget it."

"Here, watch your step." They were at the mouth of a large black-rock cave.

"I've lived in worse places," said Gabe as he stumbled across the threshold. With Karl's help he seated himself on the rocky ground with his back braced against the cave wall. "Okay, Doctor Love, your patient is ready." He looked around for the girl.

Karl stood away from him, glancing around, too. "Jan? Come on in," he said. "Jan?"

Outside the girl screamed.

CHAPTER TWELVE

The Phantom heard the scream.

It came from the direction in which the faint trail was leading him.

Must be Doctor Love, he thought, breaking into a trot.

This stretch of jungle was especially tough going. Giant wild berries grew all around, their thorny vines snaking along the ground. The thorns were knife-size, hundreds of them pronging upright.

Expertly the masked man made his way over the thorny obstacles.

Another scream came to him. Louder, more frightened, closer at hand.

After the gigantic wild berry patch came a field of grass. The blades rose up five feet. When the Phantom started into this sea of grass, a startled cricket leaped up out of his way. It was two feet long.

The Phantom ran swiftly through the chest-high grass. "Doctor Love," he called out. "Doctor Love."

He got no response.

But, after a moment, he heard the echoing crack of a pistol shot.

The Phantom ran out of the giant grass and emerged into a clearing. About a hundred feet in front of him squatted a gigantic toad. The monstrous amphibian was nearly as large as a school bus, a rough earthy brown-green in color. Its warty skin looked as tough as armorplate.

The monster toad had its great long tongue extended to almost full length and was wrapping it around the struggling body of Doctor Jan Love.

Nearby Doctor Karl Waagener was circling the creature. "Let go, damn you! Drop her!" He fired another pistol shot into the air, hoping to frighten the toad into letting go.

"The rifle," cried Jan. "Use the rifle on him."

Karl holstered his .38 pistol in his belt, dashed forward to snatch up the big-game rifle Jan had dropped. He put the butt to his shoulder and fired into the giant toad's side.

There was a loud pinging sound. The toad's enormous globe of a left eye swung slightly in Karl's direction, but otherwise the creature did not respond.

Karl got off another shot at him with similar results.

"The bullets just bounce off him. He's got a hide like iron." Angrily he turned the rifle into a club by gripping its barrel. Swinging it, he ran at the monster toad. "Let her go, damn you!"

"Get back," ordered the Phantom. One of his big .45 automatics was out of its belt holster.

The toad noticed the masked man and halted its efforts to reel in the struggling biologist.

The Phantom moved carefully toward the giant toad. He raised his automatic, aimed at one of the great globular eyes, and fired.

The toad's tongue went slack, causing Jan to lurch suddenly back into a stumbling fall.

The great amphibian toppled over, its giant knobby head slamming the ground. Almost at once enormous ants came trooping out of the foliage to attack the body.

The masked man holstered his gun as he ran to the sprawled girl. "Doctor Love, I presume?"

She sat up with his help. "Yes, I. . . ." The girl raised one hand toward her dusty face, then her eyes closed, and she started to fall over sideways.

The Phantom caught her. "Fainted," he said. "Not surprising, all things considered." He rubbed her slim wrists.

Karl was slowly approaching the masked man, his rifle held straight again. "Thanks," he said. "You saved her life and mine, too, probably. How'd you manage to drop him after my shots simply bounced off?"

"After seeing what happened when you tried to make a dent in him," explained the Phantom, "I realized the only way to kill him would be with a shot through an eye and into the brain."

"I should have thought of that," said Karl. "I'm Karl Waagener. Do you—I mean do you live here inside the volcano?"

The Phantom smiled at him. "No, I'm a tourist like yourself. I came here to locate you people."

"Then you managed to get a copter in?"

Shaking his head, the Phantom answered, "No, Karl, I climbed down from the rim."

"Climbed? But we were told that was——"

"Boy," said Jan, blinking. "What did I do, faint?"

"Yes," said Karl, taking her hand.

"Kind of a stupid feminine thing to do, wasn't it?" said the girl.

"Under the circumstances," said Karl.

"Yes, it was an awful experience. That tongue of his. I imagine that's what it must feel like when a python gets hold of you." Leaning against the Phantom she got herself to a sitting position again. "I don't know who you are, but I'm most appreciative you came along before the toad converted me into one more insect tidbit. Who are you?"

"That's not important," the Phantom told her. "I've come here looking for you."

"In a copter?"

"No."

"He climbed down," said Karl.

"He did?" Jan rose, with their help, to her feet. "That's not possible."

"Same reaction I had," said Karl.

Jan did some practice walking, her eyes on the man in the costume. "Well, I guess this is the period in my life when I'm meant to encounter a lot of things I don't believe in. Monster bees, gigantic toads and . . . now you." She glanced at her bearded associate. "Don't you realize who he must be, Karl?"

"Well, I was toying with the notion he might be——"

"Exactly," said the girl. "He's the Phantom. Aren't you?"

The Phantom made a slight acknowledging bow toward her. "What we have to do now is find a way to get out of this volcanic valley. How badly injured is your pilot?"

"How'd you——?" began Karl.

"He's the Phantom, remember," put in Jan. "He just knows."

"I found your helicopter before I found you. There were indications the pilot had been hurt."

"Yes," said Jan. "He got a pretty nasty gash when we hit the ground. After the giant bee made its suicide dive into us and fouled the rotor."

"Can he walk?" the Phantom asked.

"Certainly," said the girl. "With a little help from his friends. What do you have in mind? Do you know of a way out of here?"

The Phantom replied, "I don't think we can go out

the way I came in, especially with an injured man."
He rubbed the knuckles of one hand across his chin.
"However, I think I can find another way out."

"I have mixed feelings about leaving," said Jan.
"As a biologist, I'm fascinated by this amazing place.
Yet half the time I'm too scared even to think about
taking notes."

"Which reminds me," said the Phantom, "I believe
you dropped this." From his belt he took the notebook.

Jan's pretty face brightened. "Oh, thanks. I figured
it was gone forever. I dropped it while we were duck-
ing a swarm of mammoth mosquitoes."

"I'd better go see if Gabe needs any help." Karl
started toward the cave. "He's been pretty quiet
through all this. Hey, Gabe. Come on out and meet
our company."

There was no reply from the darkness in the rocks.

"Gabe," repeated the bearded Karl. "Hey, Gabe.
Are you okay?"

Still no answer came.

CHAPTER THIRTEEN

When the Phantom was almost at the mouth of the cave, he spotted the injured Gabe sitting erectly upright in a splash of deep shadow. "What's wrong?" the masked man asked in a low voice.

"I'm trying not to make waves," answered the pilot in a whisper. "Or much noise. I don't want to disturb this guy."

Moving silently ahead, the Phantom said, "What is it?"

"Not sure," said Gabe. "But it's three or four times bigger than me, it's got enormous teeth, and right now it's hanging upside down about thirty feet from me."

"A bat," said the Phantom softly. "A giant bat."

"It could be," agreed Gabe, whispering. "Since I noticed him, I haven't wanted to risk any quick moves. I think he's asleep up there."

Without further word, the Phantom motioned for Doctor Love and Karl to stay where they were, to remain still and silent. He climbed into the cave and slid his powerful arms under the black man. "Easy does it," he said.

"Just don't nobody sneeze," said Gabe.

The Phantom had carried Gabe not more than a dozen feet when the first tremor came.

The ground beneath them jumped and buckled like a pulled rug. Leaves, twigs, and petals came raining down. Then it was over; the earth fell still again.

"Look out," cried Jan, gesturing violently. "It's awake!"

The Phantom set Gabe on his feet and whirled round to face the giant bat.

From out of the dark cave, it came flapping, a great silent creature, black as the shadows it had left.

"Yeah, that's a giant bat sure enough," said Gabe.

"Worse than that," warned the blonde biologist. "It's *Desmodus*, the vampire bat."

"A vampire that size must get pretty thirsty," said Gabe, watching the gigantic bat go gliding up through the waning day.

"We'd better try a run for it," suggested Karl. "I'll give you a hand with Gabe."

The Phantom kept his gaze on the circling bat, on its wide snout and its vast shadowy wings. "There's no time to run. He's going to attack us."

The giant bat reached the end of its climb and wheeled. Then it came swooping down toward them.

Feet firmly planted, Jan took her rifle and sent a shot at the diving creature. "He's so darn big," she said. "It may take several shots to hit a vital spot."

The Phantom chose not to use a gun, but rather the magic spear his old friend Guran had given him.

The great vampire seemed to be after Gabe, who was leaning now on Karl's arm.

The masked man put himself between them and the swooping bat. "Guran, I hope your poison is still working," he said and hurled the spear.

The poison point passed between the enormous bat's teeth, lodged in its throat. The creature gave one strange shriek, a mixture of rage and surprise. Then came spinning, crashing, to the ground.

It missed hitting any of the four, though the tip of one wing brushed Jan's blonde hair and made it flutter like a strong wind.

Lowering her rifle, Jan approached the dead creature. "No doubt about it," she said, nodding to herself. "Vampire *Chiroptera*, a lovely specimen." She made a quick entry in her notebook.

The Phantom tugged his spear free. "Lovely," he said, "and deadly. Like a good many things here."

"Like a good many things everywhere," said the girl. "The only thing different here inside the Veiled Lady is the size of things. You see, the. . . ."

"Jan," said Karl, "we ought to get away from here. There could be more of these fellows in the neighborhood. You can lecture the Phantom when we're on safer ground."

Jan smiled. "Yes, you're right. Where to?" she asked the masked man.

The sky below the ceiling of mist was turning a very patchy blue, starting to blacken around the edges. "We'll probably be safer back in your copter, at least for tonight. In the morning, we can begin looking for a way out."

"You mean," asked Karl, "there is a way out of this valley?"

"I think there may be several," said the Phantom.

"One good one will do," said Gabe. "By the way, can one of you scientific types tell me what the earth-shaking business was all about?"

"An earth tremor," said Karl. "A mild quake."

They began moving, single file, in the direction of the downed ship.

"But this is supposed to be a dead volcano," said Gabe.

"Not dead," said Jan, "only sleeping. It's probably quite unstable."

The Phantom, who was leading the party and walking in front of the pretty blonde scientist, said, "It's odd, though. There's been no activity from the Veiled Lady for countless years. Nothing in this century as far as I know."

"That doesn't mean she couldn't still erupt," Jan told him. "Look at what happened to the volcano in the Azores Islands a few years ago. Everybody thought that one was long dead, too, until it erupted again. No, we can never be really certain with volcanos and quakes. The earth is——" She stopped herself, laughing. "That was starting to turn into another lecture. Excuse me."

Gabe, limping alongside Karl, said, "So, we can maybe expect more tremors, huh?"

"Well," said Karl, "let's say we can't rule out the possibility."

CHAPTER FOURTEEN

The next tremor came at the moment they got the campfire going.

The giant plants and flowers began to rattle and sway. Startled insects, each one as big as a baseball, went flurrying up through the fire-lit darkness. Great night birds cawed out in the blackness beyond the ruined helicopter.

The ground seemed to bounce and resound, as though an angry giant were stalking them and advancing ever nearer. The metal walls of the downed plane groaned. Enormous seedpods, hanging up in the black of the night, popped and spouted seeds like buckshot.

There was one final ripple of the ground underfoot, then the tremors ended.

The bearded Karl, who had frozen when the quakes began, resumed the motion of what he'd been doing. He bent, dropping a fresh log on the large crackling fire they'd built in the space which had been cleared around the fallen ship.

Jan, with a rueful smile, shook her head. "Looks like there'll be a slight delay on the coffee." The coffee-pot lid had popped off during the series of earth shocks, spilling coffee and water on the ground around the fire.

"We've plenty of water," said the Phantom. Earlier in the evening, he'd located a brook of drinkable water nearby. He passed a canteen to the blonde girl.

"And plenty of time to wait for it to perk," said Gabe. "We're serving an indeterminate sentence here."

"Don't be so pessimistic, Gabe," said Karl, dropping one more section of gigantic dry-weed stalk on the fire. "We've got the Phantom helping us now, remember?"

"And you got me holding you back." The pilot was sitting near the fire, his injured leg straight out in front of him. "This is our second night down inside the Veiled Lady and we're right back where we crashed."

"Your leg's looking much better," Jan reminded him while she put a new pot of coffee on the rock oven they'd constructed. "By tomorrow you should be in much better shape."

Gabe turned to watch the Phantom, who was crouched near the now-upright copter. "You really think we got a chance to get out?"

"Yes."

"How?"

"There are a couple of possibilities," said the Phantom. "I'll check those out tomorrow."

Gabe next asked Jan, "You're really ready to leave without . . . taking anything?"

The girl watched the coffee begin to perk. "Well, I suppose I would like to bring a few of these darn giant insects back with me," she admitted. "But they're too bulky to pack. Hopefully, we'll be able to make another visit to the Veiled Lady and come a little better prepared to cope."

"I don't mean insects." Gabe glanced again at the Phantom and did not continue.

Karl was holding his palms toward the fire, not because the night was cold here in the steamy volcanic valley, but simply because this was what you did with a fire you'd helped construct. "Every now and then, Gabe," he said, "I get the idea you think Jan and I are down here for some entirely different reason than the one we have. Do you?"

Gabe grinned, shaking his head. "I guess maybe I don't quite understand the scientific mind. Forget it."

"Coffee's ready," said Jan. She fished four bright-colored plastic mugs out of a knapsack. "Everybody want some?"

"None for me." The Phantom moved further away from the bright-orange glow of the fire. He stood almost in the shadowy night, straight and with arms folded.

Sipping his hot coffee, Karl said, "What about these earthquakes, Jan? I wonder if what we've felt so far is just a warmup for the big one."

Jan was kneeling on the moss, her steaming mug of coffee held in both hands. "No way of telling, Karl."

"This must be what it's like living in California," suggested Karl, "along the San Andreas fault. Waiting for the next quake to hit."

"After a while you grow indifferent," said Jan, "start thinking of other things, I'm sure." She stood, and rested her untouched cup of coffee near a wheel of the copter. "Other things such as dinner. I'll get busy with our tinned goods."

While the girl walked to the pack which held the supplies, Gabe said, "I'd like to go to California someday, when I get a little dough ahead. I hear things grow pretty big in California, too."

"Not quite this big," said Karl, laughing. "Need any help, Jan?"

The girl had selected two tins of potted meat from

their stores. "No, I can manage." Brushing back her hair with the side of her wrist, she glanced at the Phantom. The large, broad-shouldered masked man was standing almost completely in darkness now. "You do eat, don't you?"

The Phantom gave her a slight smile. "Yes, I was hoping to."

"You never know," said the girl, "with your legendary figures."

"Don't mind Jan," Karl told him. "She always kids people she likes."

After they had eaten, Karl, Gabe, and Jan retired to their makeshift bunks in the cabin of the helicopter. A tan blanket had been strung up to give Jan some privacy. Karl had suggested shifts, but the Phantom assured him he'd tend the fire through the night.

Long after midnight, a figure dropped silently from the ship.

The Phantom looked across the flickering orange fire. "You should be resting."

"I've been like this ever since I was a kid," said Jan, sitting on the ground near him. "Whenever I went on a vacation, I was always too excited to sleep the first few nights."

"And this is like a vacation to you?"

She hugged her knees, watching the flames. "In some ways, I guess," Jan said. "It's all been incredibly exciting, despite the narrow escapes. Fascinating, too. There can't be many places on the planet where life has evolved the way it has here in the valley of the Veiled Lady."

"How do you account for what's happened here?" the masked man asked her.

"Right now," the biologist replied, "I can only give

you a rough theory. But obviously the unique atmospheric conditions here inside the volcano are the cause of these mutations. Rich chemicals and gases pour from the earth. The result is that the soil and air are super-rich."

"That's what causes these giants we've been running into?"

"I'm fairly certain, yes," said Jan. "You notice so far we've seen only enlarged insects and small mammals. The combination of atmosphere and nutrition, the ecological picture, probably only works on the smaller orders of plants and animals. Don't ask me why." From a pocket, she took her black notebook and tapped it on her knee. "I think, for Gabe's sake in particular, we ought to go ahead and try to leave now."

"But you'd like to come back?"

"You're darned right, I would," replied Jan. "I want to study these giants, find out the why and wherefore." She gestured at him with the hand holding the notebook. "Suppose I can find out their secret, determine the precise combination of factors which account for this fantastic growth."

"I don't imagine you'd want to grow more giant bats."

"No, not bats, of course," she said. "But what about giant food animals, and giant vegetables and fruit? You know, I've sampled some of the berries and fruit growing here. They're perfectly all right. Now on the outside, with a forced growth or a freak giganticism you don't wind up, often, with anything too edible." She was leaning toward him. "Do you know what's lacking in the diet of so many people in the world? What's lacking right here in some of the impoverished sections of Bangalla? It's protein, both

87

meat and vegetable protein. Why, golly, if we can get at the Veiled Lady's secret, think what we could do toward feeding people. And that's only one—one! —of the more obvious applications of what's to be learned here."

"Yes," said the Phantom, "some of that had occurred to me." He was kneeling on one knee beside the fire now. "One thing which worries me, though, is——"

"The earth tremors," said the girl. "I know."

"I've lived in Bangalla for many years," the Phantom told her. "Besides which, I know much of what has happened all over Bangalla in centuries past. These quakes are something new."

"Then you think the Veiled Lady may be coming back to life?"

"I'm afraid so, yes," said the Phantom. "If she erupts while we're still down inside. . . ."

Jan sighed. "I've been afraid of the same possibility," she admitted. "What about the escape route you've spoken of?"

"Outside the volcano," said the masked man, "in the Llongo country is a river called the River of Fire."

"Yes, I've heard of it."

"The river originates here inside the Veiled Lady."

"I see," said Jan. "So if we can locate the river, we can follow it out."

The Phantom nodded. "Once we do find it, though, the journey out won't be easy. The river turns into a waterfall when it leaves the mountain and comes cascading out about a hundred feet up," he said. "But I'm fairly certain the river passes through some kind of natural cave on its way to the outside."

"Then we might possibly reach that cavern and

make our way down the outside of the volcano that way?"

"Yes, I'm counting on it," the Phantom told her. "As I've said, leaving here by the River of Fire will be difficult."

Jan asked, "Not as difficult as scaling the inside of the volcano and climbing some twelve thousand feet?"

"You and Karl seem to be in good condition," said the Phantom. "You might be able to do it, but not with Gabe."

"Then it's the river route for us," said the girl. "Maybe Gabe will be well enough tomorrow for us to begin."

The masked man said, "Tomorrow morning early, I'll take off by myself. I can travel faster alone. When I locate the River of Fire, I'll come back for you."

"Yes," agreed Jan, "that'll be a lot easier on Gabe." After a quiet moment, she said, "I think he's disappointed we're not hunting for treasure or something. Do you think there's any truth to those legends?"

"There's a grain of truth in all legends," answered the Phantom.

"Then there might really be gold and jewels here in the valley someplace?"

The masked man shook his head. "I entered the volcano from the place where the sacrifices were once made. I saw the remains of many of those unfortunate maidens. There was no sign of treasure," he said. "Perhaps no golden trinkets and rare gems were ever thrown from the bare spot. Or perhaps the ancient priests saw to it that whatever there was of value found its way to their private treasure coffers rather than to the bottom of the volcano."

The slim girl sat staring into the flames for a long

moment. "What of the legends of the Phantom?" she asked at last. "Are they all true?"

"There's a grain of truth in all legends." He had moved back away from the fire; night shadows masked the lower part of his face.

"Seems to me, I heard the Phantom has lived in these forests and jungles for centuries," said Jan. "How true is that?"

The flames made the dark shadow patterns on his face change constantly. Finally, the Phantom answered, "I've lived here most of my life."

"Have you ever been to America?"

"Yes."

"You always come back to Bangalla?"

"There's always a great deal to be done here." The masked man walked to a pile of firewood, selected two new pieces to add to the blaze. "Perhaps, it's time you turned in, Doctor."

Jan stretched her arms straight up, then rose slowly to her feet. "Why do you do all this?" she asked him.

The Phantom took her arm, leading her back to the helicopter. "Why are you a biologist?"

Jan stepped up into the dark ship. "Yes, I see."

The Phantom returned to sit beside the fire. There was a slight smile on his face.

CHAPTER FIFTEEN

When morning arrived in the volcanic valley, the Phantom was already miles from the helicopter camp. Even though he could see nothing above the fog ceiling, his acute sense of direction told him where the bare spot lay. Since he knew the River of Fire came roaring out of the mountain near where the rough-hewn stairway began, he assumed he could find the river somewhere near where he had entered the valley and trace it back.

The Phantom believed they might be able to use the river to travel across the valley, using some sort of raft. It would be much easier than hiking, with Gabe's leg still only in fair shape.

Directly ahead of the Phantom lay a vast field of bright scarlet. Some sort of wild poppies, giant in the gray morning light, swayed gently before him.

The masked man worked his way quickly through the expanse of bright, waist-high flowers. A tangle of wild grass and prickly weeds met him next. Then came a stream, a chill muddy stream. This was not the River of Fire.

Nearly across the knee-deep water, the Phantom felt something snap against his boot. Frowning at the greenish silty water, he saw something dead-white in color swirling beside his ankle. Another thump came against his leg, this time above the protective boot rim.

The Phantom felt a sharp pain flash through his leg.

He made out another large, fat deathly white shape wriggling in the water. "Leeches," he said. "Giant leeches."

He jogged, splashing, to the edge of the stream. There he jabbed at the two enormous leeches with Guran's spear. The deadly tip still contained ample poison and it did its work swiftly. In a few seconds, the two ugly hungry-mouthed creatures let go, falling, shriveling, back into the dirty flow of water.

Upon dry ground, the Phantom stopped to remove his boot and treat his minor wound. The smell of fresh blood attracted a buzzing cluster of enormous flies. The masked man had a busy ten minutes fending them off before he could resume his journey.

A few moments later, he halted again. Off to his right, he saw a grove of tough-vined flowers growing. These were the giant grail-like blossoms he had first seen outside the Veiled Lady when he began his ascent. "The river must be nearby."

Soon, except for the giant white flowers, the vegetation became more sparse. The ground took on a yellowish gritty appearance. The Phantom paused, sniffing the air. "Strong smell of sulphur," he observed.

A quarter mile more and he came to a great billowing geyser. It shot hot steamy water up out of the rocky earth. The heated water went roaring and tumbling downhill to flow in a wide river away into the distance.

"This is it then, the place where the River of Fire has its start," said the Phantom.

He made his way downhill, walking along the rocky ground at the edge of the steaming river. He reached out to test the water with a fingertip. Boiling hot he thought after a very brief immersion of his forefinger. But it looks deep enough and wide enough for boat travel. We'll just have to make sure nobody falls over-board.

The Phantom carefully blazed his route back toward Doctor Love and the others. At mid-morning, he stopped by a pool of clear water for a drink. Twined through the brush to hereabouts, he noticed a familiar, though highly enlarged, vine. The leaves were pale yellow-green, sharp-pointed. These were grape vines.

Catching hold of a low vine, the Phantom climbed up among the twists and curlicues and picked a grape. It was a smooth ripe green, about the size of a break-fast melon. The Phantom ate two grapes before dropping back to the ground. "No use stuffing myself," he said with a grin. Before he left the area he cut himself a length of tough vine.

When he came once more to the leech-filled stream, he cast the vine up and around a sturdy branch several feet over the water. After testing the strength of the improvised rope and the branch, the masked man swung smoothly over the dangerous waters.

That morning had seen another embarkation. As the dawn chill left the jungle air, Tinn, the tired-looking Chinese, was standing in a dreary clearing near the rundown Llongo country outpost. "It's not what I'd call in mint condition," he observed while he lit a new homemade cigarette and blinked at the tan-colored helicopter before him.

"It's in excellent shape," insisted Silvera. "This helicopter has served in several military operations in one of the neighboring emerging nations."

"On the losing side?"

"One hesitates to suggest you're complaining in order to postpone our departure, Tinn," said Silvera. He crossed the clearing and patted the ship. "Perhaps you'd like to radio Barber, so you can personally complain about this flying machine he's provided us with?"

"No." Tinn moved slowly toward the copter. "Why can't the guy who delivered this crate take it into the volcano?"

"Because that's not his job." Silvera climbed into the ship. "He merely works for Barber. You and I, on the other hand, have been tentatively promised an actual share of the treasure."

"When's the last time you flew one of these things?" The weary Tinn was beside the copter, looking up at Silvera.

From the pilot's seat, Silvera answered, "I'm an excellent flyer, Tinn, never fear. In my younger days I quite frequently found employment as a mercenary in various African nations. You'll be flying with an experienced combat pilot this morning. Now get on in here."

Grunting up into his seat, Tinn said, "You've never had to combat the Phantom, though. And lord knows what else is down in that hole."

Silvera began going through the pre-takeoff procedures. "One would hope you can keep your negative talk to a minimum. Don't jinx this flight, Tinn."

"It's jinxed already." Tinn buckled himself to the seat, leaving enough slack so he'd be able to slouch.

After a moment, the rotor began to revolve slowly. "I want to get clear of here before any of those savages get too curious. As it is, some of them must have heard this machine land during the night."

"You ought to be worrying about the Jungle Patrol," said Tinn. "They've been paying a lot of attention, in their own copters, to the Veiled Lady since the girl went in."

"Much too early in the day," said Silvera. "Those Jungle Patrol lads are still snug in their beds."

The helicopter shook and hummed. Then it ascended, rising over the dawn jungle.

CHAPTER SIXTEEN

The mid-morning sun sent glaring streamers of light across the deep-blue waters of the bay of Mawitaan. A brandy-colored mare whinnied and snorted as she was lifted by a sling rig out of the hold of a cargo ship. A black stevedore, hefting an enormous bale, paused to grin up at the disoriented horse. A small Oriental man in a spotless white suit was making his way along the cluttered dock, leading a low-speed red bicycle. A consignment of crated doves was being trundled away on a handtruck by a tattooed old man with a scraggly beard.

The morning air was thick with smells. Machine oil, sealife, ripening fruit, cramped livestock, exotic spices and herbs, and the sweat of hundreds of hard-working men.

Sergeant Barnum, wearing casual civilian clothes, was leaning against a whitewashed stone building at wharfside. He was finishing the last few bits of a native pastry he'd purchased in a side-street bakery, Licking glaze off his thumb and middle finger, the stocky sergeant turned his attention to the crowd around him. Barnum and Colonel Weeks had been unable to find the perpetually winking Lemos yesterday. The Jungle Patrol commander had to attend to other business this morning, but he had assigned his sergeant to continue the search for the man who'd paid the copter pilot to let Gabe McClennan take his place.

The sergeant had been roaming the Mawitaan harbor area since early morning, watching, asking questions, applying a little pressure in the right places. Leaning now against the stone building, he absently tugged a rubber band and a chain of silver paper clips out of a pocket in his wrinkled slacks. He unlinked one clip, sent it sailing toward a nearby iron post. The clip hit the post with a ping sound and Barnum smiled.

"Beautiful animals, horses." The small Oriental man with the red bike had stopped three feet in front of the sergeant and was watching the unloading of the cargo ship. He had his neat narrow white-coated back turned to Barnum. "Most beautiful."

Sergeant Barnum shot off another clip. "You want to talk to me?"

"Much more beautiful than a bicycle," continued the immaculate Oriental. "Though the bicycle is one of the aesthetic triumphs of our lamentable technological age. How much will you pay?"

"What do you have to sell?"

"You search for a certain Portuguese gentleman with an unfortunately afflicted eye," said the small Oriental, still not looking in the sergeant's direction.

"Know where he is?"

"He hides."

"I figured that out myself and it didn't cost me a penny."

"On our family plantation in Indochina we had fully one hundred horses," said the small Oriental as a struggling white stallion was lowered to the dock. "I can tell you where he hides. What is such information worth to you?"

Sergeant Barnum hefted his handful of paper clips, rattling them. "Fifteen bucks."

97

"Ha!" barked the small Oriental. He put his little hands tight on the handlebar grips. "You offer such a sum to a man who once owned a hundred fine horses?"

"All you've got now is a bicycle," said Barnum. "Twenty."

The small man's hands relaxed on the handlebars. "Twenty-five would be more satisfactory."

"Twenty is tops."

"Very well," agreed the Oriental. "I will tell you how to find him. When you leave here, please drop the money, most unobtrusively, at my feet."

"Okay, it's a deal." Barnum reached into a side pocket, put his hand on a folded wad of cash. He peeled off two tens while his big knobby hand was still in the pocket. "Where is he?"

"You are familiar with the shop of the herbologist Lee Bock?"

Barnum nodded. "Yeah. Is he there?"

"No, but Lee Bock will see that you reach his place of temporary concealment," explained the small Oriental, his narrow back still aimed at the sergeant. "You will tell him you have come to inquire about the new shipment of ginseng."

"And what's he going to soak me?"

"Nothing, nothing at all," the little man assured the Jungle Patrol sergeant.

"Okay, thanks." Sergeant Barnum squared his shoulders, and left his place against the whitewashed wall. He strolled by the cyclist, dropping the two rolled tens.

High above them another dangling horse cried out in protest.

The dirt-blurred windows of the Lee Bock Herb Emporium were filled with piles of dusty packets of roots and herbs. A large gnarled ginger root sat on a piece of patterned silk. Stuck up on all the available wall space inside the small shop were calendars, the kind of big decorative calendars shipping lines and insurance companies give away at Christmas. These calendars were from all over the world, most of them years out of date and each one showing its January page.

Lee Bock was a fat old man in a gaudy native dashiki and black-silk trousers. He had a ropy scar running along his neck and jaw; he spoke in a broken, raspy voice. "How's that again?"

"I said I'm curious about the new shipment of ginseng," repeated Sergeant Barnum, one palm resting on the narrow wooden counter which separated him from the old herb dealer.

Lee Bock frowned. "All out of ginseng, sir. I can suggest plenty of other rejuvenating herbs if that's your——"

"I was told to ask for ginseng by the man with the bicycle."

"Twenty-five bucks," said Lee Bock in his crackly voice.

"Twenty," countered Barnum.

"Absolutely not."

"Okay." The stocky sergeant gave in, dropping the cash on the worn top of the counter. He then stood jingling his handful of paper clips. "Now lead on."

"I have a bad knee. I cannot walk."

"I hear there's a herb that'll fix that."

Lee Bock gave an annoyed smile. "I will show you how to find Lemos. It is not difficult to get there, especially for one of your acuity. Look here now." He tore a length of green wrapping paper from the roll at his elbow and drew the sergeant a rough map. "That is how to reach this ancient unused warehouse. Within the building a comfortable apartment has been built. It is not a choice location perhaps, but it offers the indisputable advantage of privacy. Those, like Lemos, who wish to avoid the authorities for a time have found it an admirable place. You go through the warehouse proper, then behind this stack of mock crates you will find a concealed door. Before you go in, you must press this brick here, the fifth from the ground. Remember, the fifth up. Otherwise an alarm will sound within, alerting your quarry. Is all this clear to you?"

"Yeah," replied Barnum as he was handed the rough map.

The Jungle Patrol sergeant followed Lee Bock's instructions, and in fifteen minutes he was in the old warehouse, standing before the door behind the stack of large wooden boxes.

He counted bricks and leaned down to tap the correct one. He drew his pistol from beneath his shirt and nudged the door open. The door swung inward to reveal a corridor lit only by the light which made its way down through a grimy skylight.

There was another door at the corridor's end. Pistol in hand, the sergeant charged that door. He kicked it open, dived through.

He landed, however, not in a hideout apartment, but at the bottom of a black pit.

CHAPTER SEVENTEEN

The helicopter was coming erratically down, bobbing and drifting like a feather in the wind.

Tinn was sitting upright in his seat, his cigarette unlit between his lips. "What's the matter?" he asked once again.

"I told you, the air currents are crazy inside this damn volcano." Silvera's dark face was speckled with perspiration; his hair had an extra curl to it.

"This is what killed Gabe," said Tinn.

"Be quiet," Silvera told him, struggling to keep the helicopter under his control.

They had reached the rim of the Veiled Lady nearly twenty minutes ago and entered the hollow mountain with little trouble. Now, with the heavy mist rubbing at their ship and the great gusts of hot air wooshing up from below, the copter was growing more and more difficult to control.

"Why is it making that noise?" asked Tinn.

"What noise?"

"That noise."

The copter was giving off a loud chattering sound as it swayed unevenly on the odd air currents within the volcano. Then it suddenly dropped, with a plummeting abruptness, several hundred feet straight down.

When Silvera got control of the ship again, his head began swinging rapidly from side to side as he rechecked all the instruments spread out before him. "Our radar setup isn't working," he said.

"You told me this crate was in A-1 shape," reminded the Chinese.

"Quiet."

The copter rocked, jerking down unevenly through the thick mist.

Silvera muttered to himself in his mother tongue. "It feels as though the Veiled Lady were taking over control of the ship," he said.

The helicopter swung sharply to the left. The rotating blades all at once gave off a terrific rackety noise. Then a huffing, puffing sound.

Tinn's head was tilted far back. "You ran into something."

The propellers ceased turning. The sway and drift ended as the helicopter began falling earthward.

"Some kind of bird you hit," gasped the Chinese.

Abruptly the ground met them. There was a gigantic slam.

Tinn's teeth clacked together. His handmade cigarette exploded and sent flecks of tobacco spinning through the still-vibrating cabin.

Silvera was slumped in the pilot's seat, held partially upright by his safety belts.

The Chinese rubbed at his head, wiped at his eyes. Then he turned to look at his partner. "Hey, Silvera, are you okay?"

The little dark man groaned.

Tinn got himself unfastened and reached over to poke Silvera. "Anything broken? Are you badly hurt?"

Groaning again, Silvera's eyes flickered. "What?"

"How are you?"

"One would imagine the crash was not serious enough to do any great damage," said Silvera. "Apparently we were much closer to the ground than our instruments indicated."

"How about the radio?" asked Tinn. "Is it working?"

Silvera wiped his sweaty forehead with the back of his hand. "I'll try it," he said. "I hate to admit botching the final stages of this flight, but, nonetheless, we'll need help getting out of here."

"I doubt Barber's going to put any more planes or people in here."

Silvera was working at the radio. It did not respond. After several minutes, he announced, "She's dead. The impact caused that."

Tinn let out a heavy sigh. "So here we are at the bottom of the volcano, marooned like Crusoe and Friday."

"Let's not despair, Tinn," said Silvera. "There are several possibilities which suggest themselves to the— my god!"

"Huh?"

The little dark man's eyes had turned toward the partially shattered window of the cabin. He was pointing now at something outside. "The mist doesn't exist down here close to the ground," he said. "I just realized one could see out there. Look there, Tinn."

A flock of angry flies was circling the ship. Each fly was as large as a flying squirrel. Their buzzing was incredibly loud.

"Flies," said Tinn. "Why do they look so big? Is it a distortion of the glass?"

"I'd like to think so," said Silvera. "I'm afraid not, however."

One of the huge flies had landed on the glass, was walking over it, its great many-faceted blue-green eyes watching Silvera.

"Do you think," asked Tinn, watching the fly intently, "those things are an exception? Or do you think——"

"One has to seriously consider the possibility there will be other such overgrown life-forms down here."

Tinn slumped down into his seat, eyes never leaving the droning giant flies. "It's . . . it's incredible," he said finally. "What . . . what possibly can have caused it?"

"You'll have to save that question for the good Doctor Love."

"What are we going to do now? It's not possible to go out there."

"Oh, yes, it's highly possible," corrected Silvera. "Unless you'd like to die right here in this plane."

"We've got supplies. We can stay in here, live on that until somebody sends a rescue party."

"You forget that the only somebody who knows we're here is Barber," reminded Silvera. "He's not likely, as you yourself suggested, to invest any further time or money in this project. So after we've eaten up our supplies, we'll be finished."

"I don't see as how there's any alternative."

"There are always alternatives," said Silvera. "I intend to locate Doctor Love and take the treasure away from her. While I'm at it, I'll also determine if Gabe is still on our side."

"Dead is what he probably is," said Tinn sadly. "A meal for a big bug."

"I doubt that. I don't think we'll have that much trouble either," said Silvera. "Our guns can handle most anything, big or small, we're liable to encounter."

Tinn said, "Okay, suppose we do go out there? Suppose we find the treasure. What then? We're still stuck eight thousand feet down inside a volcano."

The small dark Silvera said, "You're forgetting the Phantom."

"No, I just put him at the back of my mind while I worried about our latest troubles."

"He did not fly in; he climbed," said Silvera. "One now has at least two possibilities to consider. First, it may well be possible to climb out the way the Phantom climbed in. Second, it may also be possible the Phantom knows another way out."

"We simply walk up to him and ask?"

"Yes," said Silvera, chuckling, "being sure we have a rifle or two pointed at him."

Tinn finally began rolling himself a cigarette. "I find none of those prospects pleasing."

"Be that as it may, you'll go along," Silvera told him. "Come, let's get started."

A moment later the small dark man was standing on the mossy turf of the volcanic valley.

CHAPTER EIGHTEEN

Jan Love glanced up, then dropped the tin of bacon she'd been about to open. "Karl," she called out in a faint voice.

Stepping out of the giant vegetation beyond the clearing were two men. The one in the lead was small and dark. He carried a Winchester rifle casually under his right arm. The second man was a heavyset Chinese, with a .45 automatic in his fist, who looked very much in need of sleep. When the Chinese stepped into the clearing his left elbow brushed a tall weed stalk, causing enormous umbrellalike seeds to come spiraling down through the morning.

"What is it?" said Karl, peering out of the copter cabin. "Why, it's a rescue."

"I don't think so," said Jan as the little man's rifle swung to cover Karl.

"One mustn't judge by appearances," said Silvera, with a little smile. "We might very well be your saviors."

Jan went two paces backward as they approached. "How did you get down here into the Veiled Lady?"

Tinn answered her. "Same way you did, by copter."

"Then you could fly us out?"

"If the lousy crate hadn't smashed on landing," said Tinn.

Silvera had crossed to the copter. His rifle barrel inscribed a small arc as he gestured with it. "Come down out of there, Doctor Waagener. And where's this Phantom fellow?"

"Who?" asked Karl.

"Drop on down here," ordered Silvera. "One would advise you not to try conning us. We know the Phantom came into the volcano."

"Perhaps he did," said Jan, "but we haven't seen him." If she could convince them the Phantom was nowhere around it might give the masked man a better chance of taking this pair by surprise when he returned.

"Is that so, Gabe?" Silvera called into the copter.

After a silent twenty seconds, Gabe answered, "No, they're trying to cover for him. He was here, but he's out in the wilds hunting now."

"Gabe!" said Jan.

His eyes and gun on the blonde girl, Tinn said, "You're not dead, huh, Gabe?"

"No, only a little banged up." The pilot climbed out of the ship, favoring his injured leg.

"See," said Silvera. "This place isn't as bad as you thought, Tinn. It didn't kill Gabe."

"Bad enough," said Tinn. "Gabe, you ought to see what we had to fight our way through while we've been hunting for you. Giant things, everything's giant. Bugs, insects, birds. What in——?"

"Save the biology for later," said Silvera. "How come we didn't hear from you, Gabe?"

Slowly Gabe drew out his pistol. "The radio went out when we crashed." He motioned Silvera off, turning his snub-nosed .32 pistol on Karl. "I can watch him."

The bearded Karl frowned. "What is this, Gabe?"

Laughing, Silvera said, "What it is, is we outfoxed you, Professor. Gabe is our boy."

"But why?" Jan wanted to know.

"Can't you guess?" asked Tinn.

"No," said Jan, watching Gabe's face. "What's this all about, Gabe?"

Silvera strode toward her. "It's about a fortune in gold and gems, which we've come to relieve you of."

"What?" said Karl.

Silvera turned toward Gabe. "Where have they got the loot stashed, Gabe?"

"Well, now," said Gabe, "that's just it, Silvera. They haven't."

"What in the hell are you talking about?" demanded Silvera.

"Maybe," suggested the weary-eyed Tinn, "he's decided to double-cross us."

"I'm telling you there's no treasure," said Gabe. "They haven't got it."

"Then where the hell is it?" asked Silvera.

Gabe shrugged. "I don't know."

"You don't know? You don't know? You've been down here for days and you don't know. What did they do with it?"

"Nothing," said Gabe. "There is no treasure."

"No treasure? Of course there's a treasure," said the little dark man. "That's why they came down here, because they knew where it was. Why would they risk their hides otherwise?"

Jan smiled evenly at the angry Silvera. "We ventured into the Veiled Lady for one reason only: to study the mutated life-forms we suspected might exist down here."

"Oh, I've heard all about that." Silvera moved closer to the girl. "That's the story you made up to fool those idiots on the Jungle Patrol. Don't think you can use it to fake us out."

"Look," put in Gabe, "I think she's telling the truth, Silvera."

"Oh, do you?" Silvera gave him a twisted smile. "Well, I don't think she is, and neither would Barber. He didn't get where he is by making bad guesses."

"I've been with them around the clock," insisted Gabe. "They have never even mentioned the treasure. They really are biologists, like they say."

Tinn took a deep careful drag of his newest home-made cigarette. "What did you do, boy, give away your cover? They must have got wise to you. That's why they've kept quiet."

"Damn it," said Gabe. "You guys have made a mistake—you and Barber, too. There's no treasure. Forget it and concentrate on how we get out of here."

"First things first," said Silvera.

Karl asked Gabe, "Suppose we hadn't crashed and there actually was a treasure? What was the plan?"

"There's no treasure. Never mind what the plan was."

Silvera chuckled. "One must admit our original plan was excellent, and vastly simpler than what we're now engaged in."

Karl asked, "You intended to fly out with the treasure and leave us here?"

"Exactly," answered Silvera.

"Oh, Gabe," said Jan in a soft faraway voice.

"Now we have had enough chitchat and confessional sessions," said Silvera. "I want to know where the treasure is." He had eased up to within inches of Jan. "I would appreciate being told."

Jan looked down to meet his gaze. "There is no treasure."

Silvera slapped her across the cheek. "I do not enjoy being lied to."

"You'd better not try that again!" shouted Karl.

Tinn pointed his automatic in Karl's direction. "No heckling."

"There is no treasure," repeated the girl.

Silvera slapped her twice more.

"Damn you," said Karl.

"Leave her alone," said Gabe.

Silvera scowled at the pilot. "Don't tell me what to do, boy." He reached out suddenly to slap Jan again.

"I'm telling you," warned Gabe. "Leave her alone."

Silvera caught hold of Jan's long blonde hair, tugged and twisted it, pulling her head down closer to his. "Tell us now."

Gabe made a rumbling, roaring sound in his throat. He came across the clearing in a hobbling run. "Let go of her, man," he said. He kicked out with his good leg, catching Silvera in the kneecap hard with his boot toe.

"Hey!" The dark little man hopped back. He swung his rifle up, aimed it straight at Gabe.

Gabe's finger squeezed the trigger of his .32.

A slug dug into Silvera's right arm near the shoulder. He screamed, dropped to his knees, but kept hold of his rifle.

Gabe dived into the surprised and stunned Tinn. He hit the Chinese's low-hanging stomach with an elbow. Fresh blood was staining the leg of Gabe's trousers. His wound had opened again. "Run," he told Jan. "Get the Phantom."

The wounded Silvera was swinging his rifle up again.

Jan turned, sprinted into the giant underbrush. After a moment, she heard another shot. She didn't know if it had been aimed at her or Gabe.

She kept running.

CHAPTER NINETEEN

Jan had the impression she was jogging through a giant's garden. All around her grew wild cabbage, the heads as large as compact cars, the enormous veined leaves a glaring sea-green. She had been running for well over ten minutes. There was no sound of pursuit; no sound at all came to her from back at the campsite.

The lovely blonde slowed to a walk, then stopped entirely. "Get hold of yourself, old girl," she said. She was breathing rapidly, her mouth open. "If you're going to find the Phantom, you're going to need a plan."

She began walking, passing wild kale with curly tipped leaves the size of shop awnings. "The River of Fire should run toward the south of the volcano, he told me, toward the place where they built that sacrificial platform so long ago. So the Phantom probably went south."

Jan changed her course. Presently she was making her way through fields of gigantic weeds. The morning grew warmer; the high ceiling of mist took on a more yellow tinge from the unseen sun.

Gradually, somewhere behind her, a clattering sound started. After a moment, Jan turned her head to see what was making the noise. "Golly, a member of the family *Manitidae!*" exclaimed the girl biologist.

Tottering toward her through the high weeds was a praying mantis. This one was almost six feet tall, thin, green, with waving antennae and red globular

111

eyes. It looked, with its lean spikey forefeet and elongated many-jointed body, like some fantastic mechanical construction, some robot programmed to follow Jan.

"They call the mantis the tiger of the insect world," she recalled, edging sideways. "He's a highly carnivorous fellow."

The giant mantis adjusted its course so that it was still heading right for her.

The enormous creature had assumed the bent, supplicating posture which gave it its name. The praying position which always proceeded the mantis's attack on its prey.

Turning her back on the thing, Jan ran.

It straightened and came shambling after her.

The girl was several yards ahead of the pursuing mantis when her ankle got caught in a loop of ground-running vine. Her body jerked, then she fell straight forward, landing hard among some nettles. The sharp thorns dug into her bare arms as she twisted round to face the approaching carnivorous mantis.

"Darn it," said Jan. "No gun and very little chance to run."

She began to shout at the insect while she fought to disentangle herself from the prickly vines all around her. "Go away, darn you!"

The mantis was praying once again, preparing to make a spiky grab at her.

A second later the gigantic insect stiffened, snapped upright to its full six-foot length. Its antennae drooped. It started to rock from side to side. A few seconds more and the mantis toppled over to lie dead in the thorns.

Jan saw the Phantom standing immediately behind the spot where the praying mantis had been. In his powerful hands he held his spear. "Remind me," said Jan, "to get the recipe for that poison."

"I don't think Guran will part with it." The masked man reached out a hand to her. "Careful now; easy does it."

"How'd you get here?"

"Heard you shouting."

Jan, on her feet, brushed back her blonde hair and examined the tears in her blouse. "I'm glad," she said.

"And what are you up to, Doctor Love?"

The girl took a deep breath before answering. "I was coming to find you."

"Why, what's the trouble?"

Jan said, "It's incredible, but somehow two men walked into our camp this morning. Two men with guns."

"What? How did they get here?"

"Copter," answered Jan. "Don't get your hopes up, though; their ship crashed, too."

"You wouldn't be running from a Jungle Patrol rescue team," said the Phantom. "Who are these men?"

"Their names are . . . Silvera and Tinn. Silvera is a small, swarthy, nasty man, the other one's a pudgy Chinese. I think they said they worked for a man named . . . named Barber."

The Phantom nodded. "Yes, I've heard of Barber, and some of his activities. Why would a crook like Barber be interested in a scientific project such as yours?"

"Apparently this Barber has the notion we came down here to find the treasure of the Veiled Lady."

"He sent these two to hijack you?"

"Yes," said Jan. "But not only that. He hired Gabe to be a—well, a spy for him."

"So that's why Gabe kept wondering why you weren't looking for treasure."

"Wait though." She put her hand on his arm. "I think Gabe has had a change of heart."

"How so?"

"Well, you see, the little one, Silvera, got the idea he'd find out where the treasure was if he hit me a few times."

The Phantom's fingers tightened into fists. "He did, did he?"

"That made Karl and Gabe unhappy," continued Jan. "Gabe, being supposedly on their side, had a gun. Well, what he did was shoot Silvera and tell me to run for it."

The Phantom asked, "So how many do we have to worry about encountering in the camp?"

"I'm not sure. Silvera was hurt, but still had control of his Winchester when I left. Which could mean there are still two armed men there."

"Or possibly three if Gabe's had another change of heart."

"I don't think so. I think he's on our side for good now."

"We'll soon find out," the Phantom told her.

CHAPTER TWENTY

Colonel Weeks came pounding down the front steps of the Jungle Patrol headquarters building. A tall black man in the uniform of the Mawitaan police was approaching up the path. "Any news, Lieutenant Kiwanda?" called out the colonel.

"I think perhaps, yes," answered the police lieutenant.

"You know where Sergeant Barnum is?" The sergeant had not reported in for several hours, and the colonel, worried, had called on the Mawitaan police for assistance in finding out what might have happened.

"Not exactly where he is," answered Lieutenant Kiwanda, "but where he was something like an hour ago. We can drive there and talk to the street police man who believes he noticed your Sergeant Barnum."

"Yes, very well." Colonel Weeks followed the lieutenant to a tan-colored Volkswagen. "Where is it?"

Starting the car, Lieutenant Kiwanda said, "My man says he saw the sergeant enter Bahari Lane earlier this morning. He did not see him leave. Bahari Lane is a dead end, as you know."

While they drove toward the Mawitaan waterfront, the Jungle Patrol commander said, "Yes, that's right. So Barnum may still be on that block somewhere."

"It lies in a not too-reputable sector," said the policeman. "That particular lane is mostly uninhabited except for a few nondescript shops and some abandoned buildings."

"He's trying to get a lead on the whereabouts of Lemos," said the colonel. "Anything to tie Lemos in with Bahari Lane?"

"Lemos could be tied in with most anything." The lieutenant turned onto a curving street from which they could see the broad Mawitaan harbor. "Now and then, one or another of those gutted apartment houses on Bahari is used as a rendezvous spot for narcotics dealers and their unfortunate customers. We try to discourage that, but, you know. . . ."

"Not enough men," supplied Weeks. He grew silent, dipping the bowl of his pipe into his tobacco pouch.

Lieutenant Kiwanda stopped the VW to allow a fruit vendor to push a cart of melons and pineapples from one side of the narrow street to the other. "Why exactly do you want to see Lemos?"

"You've heard about what happened to Doctor Love and her party, haven't you?"

"The lady scientist who was lost in the Veiled Lady, yes. What has Lemos to do with that?"

"We want to ask him," said the gray-haired colonel, "for the reason he was anxious to make sure he got a certain pilot to take their helicopter into the volcano."

"Which pilot would that be?" The black police lieutenant pulled up to a curb. "The lane is nearby. Let us walk."

Stretching up out of the little tan car, Colonel Weeks said, "The pilot Lemos planted on the flight was Gabe McClennan."

"Ah, yes, Gabe. I was hoping he'd straighten out as he matured."

"So was I," said the colonel.

The foot patrolman was not in evidence at the

116

moment. "My patrol corporal seems to be elsewhere," said Kiwanda. "We'll look over the little street ourselves."

They turned down a small shadowy lane.

Seated on a crate in front of a narrow fly-infested grocery was a huge black woman in a loose gown of bright silk. Large round discs of deep-green glass covered her eyes. She was chewing on a tiny brownish apple. "Good morning, Lieutenant."

"Good morning, Mother Mafuta."

"Have you seen a broad, stocky man go by here?" the colonel asked the fat woman.

She tapped the right lens of her dark spectacles with chunky fingertips. "I don't see anything, ever."

"But you hear," suggested Lieutenant Kiwanda.

Mother Mafuta grinned, taking another small bite of her apple. "I heard a lumbering fellow, with booted feet, go by an hour or so ago."

"Any idea where he headed?"

"All the way down the lane, to the end. Either into that warehouse nobody uses any more, or on through the alley and jumped into the bay."

"Thank you, mother," said Lieutenant Kiwanda.

Colonel Weeks was already hurrying toward the warehouse the fat shopkeeper had indicated. The building was low, a smeary black in color. The wide wooden front door stood open an inch.

Lieutenant Kiwanda kicked it gently open with his foot.

A dim silence greeted them inside.

"Look there," said the colonel, pointing at the warehouse floor with the stem of his pipe. "That floor's been recently swept with a pushbroom."

"So it has." The lieutenant had his hand on his holster as they entered the dim place.

117

A jumble of rusted machinery lay to the immediate right of the doorway. At the other end of the low, flat-ceilinged room were piled several dozen wooden crates. You could hear the waters of the bay lapping at the pilings out behind the building. Sunlight made its way through the small dirty skylights, catching motes of dust and making them glitter for an instant.

Colonel Weeks's eyebrows went up and down. "What's that?" He trotted over near the packing cases, bent to scoop up something in his hand. He'd seen it flash in the sunlight. It was a metal paper clip. He scanned the immediate area, then pushed his way in between the boxes.

The policeman followed him. "You've found something?" he asked.

The colonel was hunkered in front of a narrow door in the wall. Three more paper clips, linked in a chain, lay on the floor. "Fooling around with paper clips is a habit of Barnum's," he explained. He pocketed these, stood, and inclined his head toward the door. "Let's find out what's on the other side of that."

While the colonel flattened himself against the stone wall to the left of the door, Lieutenant Kiwanda kicked it open.

There was no one in the corridor beyond the door. After about three seconds, someone down at the corridor's end said, "What the hell was that?"

"I don't know."

"Go see."

Kiwanda was in the shadowy hall, running toward the voices. Colonel Weeks was close behind him.

The door at the end of the corridor snapped open and the top half of a husky black man showed. He was standing on a staircase, apparently. He held a pistol in his hand. Recognizing Lieutenant Kiwanda, he said, "How do you do, Lieutenant?"

"I'm doing very well, thank you," replied the policeman. "Will you put down the gun?"

The husky man blinked at the weapon in his hand as though he'd never seen it before. "Yes, sorry." He reached up to place the pistol carefully on the hall floor.

"We'd like to see what's happening down there." Lieutenant Kiwanda strode ahead and picked up the surrendered weapon.

"Not much to see, Lieutenant. An old rundown pier, lots of rats. Matter of fact, that's why I had the gun, for shooting rats."

"Even so," said Lieutenant Kiwanda.

The big black man backed down the staircase.

Below was a scummy wooden dock built out over the bay water on bowlegged pilings. A swayback roof covered most of the ramshackle dock.

"Oh, just the man I want to see!" exclaimed a large man down on the pier. He wore a blue suit, complete with vest. His left eye seemed to be winking at them. At his feet, bound and gagged, lay Sergeant Barnum.

"Yes, I'm sure," said Kiwanda.

Colonel Weeks went down the rickety steps two at a time, and ran to his sergeant's side. "He's alive," he said, pulling out a pocket knife.

"Why, bless my soul," said the blue-suited Lemos, "of course he is. I was about to rush out to phone the police, Lieutenant Kiwanda. You can imagine my surprise when I arrived to inspect this shabby out-of-repair property of mine, at finding this complete stranger on——"

"Shut up," ordered the colonel. He had all the ropes off Barnum.

The stocky sergeant sat up, ripped off the handkerchief gag. "They were going to heave me into the bay soon as it got dark," he said.

"On the contrary," insisted the winking Lemos. "We were merely playing a joke. We mistook this gentleman for a prowler and decided to have a little sport with him."

"Lemos didn't expect to get caught for a few days yet," said the sergeant. "He's expecting some money which will enable him to travel far from Mawitaan."

"Money from where?" asked the colonel.

"Seems like there's a treasure at the bottom of the volcano," said Barnum. "Lemos here stands to get a piece of it."

The colonel took hold of Lemos's vest. "Why did you want Gabe McClennan to fly that plane?"

Lemos held both palms toward the angry colonel, shook them negatively. "I am not the master planner of this grand design, Colonel," he said. "I am only a cog in the wheel."

"Who makes the wheel go round?" the colonel wanted to know, his grip tightening. "What does it have to do with Doctor Love?"

"Perhaps you had best put those questions to the man who hired me." Lemos's left eye closed completely.

"Who is he?"

Lemos hesitated, then said, "Barber. He is Barber who owns and operates the Scarlet Cockatoo."

Colonel Weeks let go of the man. Turning to Sergeant Barnum, he asked, "You up to paying a visit to Barber?"

"That I am," the sergeant assured him.

CHAPTER TWENTY-ONE

"Careful," warned the Phantom in a low voice. "Someone's heading this way." With a swift silent motion of his right hand, he drew out one of his .45 automatics.

Jan crouched beside the masked man in a tangle of wild grass. They were fairly near the campsite. "Another darn mantis?"

Up ahead the chest-high grass swayed and rattled. The Phantom shook his head. "Human."

The dry, thrashing sound rose in intensity. Then a voice called out, "Jan, where are you, Jan?"

"It's Karl," exclaimed the girl, starting to her feet.

The Phantom pushed her back down, cautioning, "They may be using him to decoy you out into the open. Wait right here; don't show yourself until I come for you." As he spoke, he unholstered his other black automatic and handed it to her. "I believe you know how to use one of these."

"Yes, I do."

Suddenly the Phantom was gone. He moved away through the high grass noiselessly.

The blonde girl knelt and waited, the .45 automatic resting on her palm. Overhead a swarm of gnats, the size of golf balls, were hovering.

"Jan, everything's okay," called Karl. "You can come on back. Jan?"

A moment later the Phantom returned. "It's all right," he said.

"Karl, over here!" shouted Jan as she stood to wave at him.

The bearded biologist came running toward her. "You can come back. Gabe and I have taken care of them and——hey! You found the Phantom."

"He found me." Jan took Karl by the hand. "In the nick of time, too. I'll explain later. First tell us what happened back in camp."

"Well, the little diversion caused by your departure gave me the opportunity to jump Tinn," explained Karl. "Meantime Gabe was tangling with the other guy. He got shot again."

"Gabe?"

"No, Silvera," said Karl. "He's dead."

Jan asked, "Is Gabe okay?"

"The gash on his leg tore open again," answered Karl. "I treated it and bandaged it before coming to hunt for you. I think he'll make it."

"Are you certain," asked the Phantom, "you can trust Gabe now?"

Karl turned toward the masked man. "Yes, I am. I think Gabe realizes he made a mistake ever tying up with those boys. When the time came to make a decision, Gabe chose to side with us."

"Yes," Jan told the Phantom, "we can trust Gabe; I'm certain."

"Very well," he said.

Karl asked, "Did you locate the River of Fire?"

"Yes. We can start for there shortly," said the Phantom. "First we'll gather up the rest of the party back at camp. And see what we can do about the dead man." He turned and began walking in the direction from which Karl had come.

"The river is boiling hot, isn't it?" asked Karl, following with Jan at his side. "Seems like a pretty wild idea to float out of here on a boiling river."

"It's worth a try," said Jan. "It's probably our only chance of getting out. But we'll need a raft."

"I have an idea about that," said the Phantom.

Before they reached the fallen helicopter, another series of tremors began to shake the earth. They were the most severe shocks yet, causing the ground to bounce and rumble, shaking and thrashing the giant vegetation. The tremors didn't stop so soon this time. They continued for minutes, subsided, then began again.

"I don't like this," said Jan, holding tight to Karl's arm to maintain her balance.

"Do you think," asked the Phantom, "it may mean there's going to be a volcanic eruption?"

They reached, at last, the campsite clearing. "Well, I'm a biologist, not a geologist," said the girl. "But I would say it doesn't look good."

"What's going to happen now?" Tinn wanted to know. He was on the ground on his hands and knees.

Gabe was standing near him. He had Tinn's automatic stuck in his waistband, his own pistol in his hand. "Think she's going to blow?"

"It's possible," replied Jan. "It's possible." The ground had ceased to shake.

"The Phantom has found a way out," announced Karl. "We'll be leaving soon."

"How?" asked Gabe. "By way of that river?"

"Yes," said the masked man.

"What the world needs now," said the black man, "is a boat."

"I think," said the Phantom, "we should be able to use the body of your helicopter as a raft. We won't have time to build a boat from scratch."

"The thing's too heavy," Gabe pointed out.

"Not if we strip it!" The masked man leaped into the ship. "We'll have to dump the engine, all the equipment. Give me a hand, Karl."

"Soon as I take care of the remains of Silvera," answered Karl.

Gabe motioned to Jan. "You watch this guy Tinn and I'll help out in the copter."

"You shouldn't, Gabe. Your leg. . . ."

"I won't need either leg if we get buried in lava." He gave her his pistol and went hobbling to the ship.

"I still don't understand this place," complained Tinn. "It's full of giant bugs. It's likely to explode and cover us all with lava. And the rivers are full of boiling water. I don't understand this place."

"I'll explain while we're waiting," offered Jan.

Gradually at first, almost gently, the ground had begun to shake again. This time it didn't stop.

They were nearly to the River of Fire. Karl and Tinn were pushing the gutted copter. The Phantom, his powerful muscles barely straining, was pulling, using new vine ropes he'd fashioned before they departed the camp. Jan and Gabe, who was limping badly, walked alongside the makeshift raft.

"The big eruption must be coming," said Karl. "The ground is shaking like jello."

Jan glanced upward. "All the wildlife seems to sense it."

Monster bees roared overhead like a flight of bombers. Gigantic butterflies flapped by, all seeking escape and safety, none sure in which direction it lay.

"Maybe we ought to hitch a ride with one of those guys," suggested Gabe with a grin. "They're probably going to fly right up out of the Veiled Lady."

"No," said Jan, shaking her head, "those poor creatures need the special atmosphere down here in order to survive. The ordinary air of our world's too thin for them. Which is why they've never flown outside before—why no one knows about them."

"Then they'll all die," said Gabe, "if this thing blows."

"Yes, I'm afraid so," Jan said.

"To hell with the big bugs," said Tinn. "We're the ones who're going to die in here."

The ground tremors were becoming more severe. All around giant plants and bushes were swaying, branches breaking off to come spinning down. Blossoms, leaves, seedpods, thorns showered on them. The land trembled and shook like a giant in agony.

"There's the River of Fire," said the Phantom.

In a few hard-working minutes, they got the copter-raft into the water. Resting on its side, it floated well. Even when the five of them carefully climbed aboard, the ship stayed afloat. Using the detached rotor blades as paddles, the Phantom and Karl got the rude raft moving downstream.

"Well, here we go," said Jan.

"And so we bid a fond farewell to the fabulous land of the Veiled Lady," said Gabe.

"What's so funny?" asked Tinn. "You didn't get any treasure, not a bit. And we'll be damn lucky if we get out of this place alive. Don't you realize that?"

No one answered him.

CHAPTER TWENTY-TWO

A frightened dragonfly, looking like a World War I airship, flew over, almost touching their heads. A huge black spider came floating by, dead in the boiling hot current of the River of Fire. The giant growth along the shoreline was waving, whipping as though facing a hurricane. The rumbling of the quivering earth was louder.

"Hey!" said Karl. He left off paddling for a moment, pointing ahead with a blistered hand. "We're coming to a cavern."

"That should take us through the side of the mountain," said the Phantom. "Remember that the river shoots out a hundred feet above the ground outside. We have to keep the current from carrying us right over the falls."

"How are we going to do that?" asked Gabe.

Nodding at the coils of vine rope lying on the copter side next to him, the Phantom explained, "We're going to have to lasso some rocks and anchor our raft that way. Then we'll see about climbing down the mountainside without getting boiled."

"None of this," said the weary-looking Tinn, "is going to work."

The current grew stronger and Karl and the Phantom used their paddles only to control the course of the ship.

They left the last of the light, and floated into the darkness of the great rock cavern.

Stretching out flat on his stomach, Gabe reached down into the cabin. "Here's a couple of big flashlights we can use." He kept one and handed the other over to Jan.

Tinn asked the girl, "Doctor Love, what if this volcano erupts? There'll be lava, won't there? It'll start flowing."

"Yes, it will."

"It'll flow this way, won't it? Downhill along the course of this lousy river."

Jan answered, "Yes, there's a good possibility the cave will fill with lava instead of water."

"I'm glad I didn't bet with anybody on my chances of getting out of here alive."

Gabe clicked on his flashlight, played its beam on the walls of the great cavern. The rock sides were jagged, a blue-black metallic color. Enormous splotches of pale-orange fungus dotted the walls. "Not too cheerful," he said. "But at least nobody's written their names on the walls."

The waters of the River of Fire sputtered and hissed as the copter-raft made its way through the rocky darkness.

"I wonder why some of the giant insects don't come into this cave for safety," said Karl. "Haven't seen one."

"I wouldn't complain about that," muttered Tinn.

Jan swung her flashlight up to study the ceiling of the cavern. "I don't know, Karl. Maybe they've got a reason for shying away."

From behind them came a series of explosive booms. The cave walls quivered, boiling water splashed high up against the sides of the floating copter.

"Wow!" said Gabe. "It's getting worse."

"We're never going to make it," said Tinn. "This whole damn mountain is going to fall in on us."

The Phantom and Karl kept up their use of the paddles. The raft was making good time along the hot river.

The explosions back in the valley were coming closer together, echoing and bouncing off the jagged walls of the cavern.

"Something up ahead," said Gabe. He aimed his light in the direction they were floating. "My god!"

"What—what's that?" exclaimed Karl.

Jan joined her flashlight beam with Gabe's. "It's an enormous lizard of some sort."

Filling the cave twenty feet ahead of them was a gigantic scaly creature. It was a blotchy black and green in color with a short stubby head, wide-clawed feet. Its large mouth was filled with spiky teeth which seemed to be grinning at them. It had a huge forked tongue that was hissing out at them, almost touching the raft.

The Phantom and Karl halted the progress of their craft.

"It's like some sort of gila monster," said Jan. The hand holding the flashlight on the monster was steady. "Big as an ancient dinosaur."

"I wonder if it's poisonous like the gila monster," said Karl.

"Stop all this scientific stuff!" cried Tinn. "Let's get the hell out of here." He was standing upright, causing the copter body to sway.

"Sit down, you're rocking the boat," Gabe told him.

"You're not going to feed me to that thing." Tinn scrambled toward the rear of the craft. "Come on, come on. Let's back up."

"This is the only way out of here," said Karl. "Now sit down."

"Look at that creature's eyes," said Jan, gesturing with the flashlight. "They're closed tight."

"He's probably blind," said the Phantom. Resting his paddle, he drew out one of his automatics. "I imagine he's got a keen sense of smell and hearing." Taking careful aim the Phantom fired at the monster lizard.

"Your bullets don't even phase him," said Jan. "Even when you hit his eye. They just bounce off."

"There's no chance of stopping him," said Tinn. "He's going to get us all." He was standing at the back edge of the copter.

"Sit down," warned Gabe.

"I'm not waiting to get eaten!" said Tinn. The sad-faced Chinese leaped from the raft.

"Tinn, that water's boiling hot!" shouted Gabe, making a futile grab.

The Chinese screamed once before he sank beneath the bubbling surface of the River of Fire.

"Oh, my lord!" said Jan.

"He panicked," said Gabe. "I tried to catch him, but with this damn leg. . . ."

"It's not your fault," said Jan.

The Phantom kept his attention on the giant lizard. "Okay," he said, "let's see what the poison spear will do to this fellow."

"You've had good luck with it so far," said Karl.

The great lizard was creeping closer, its huge tongue whipping at them.

"There!" The Phantom hurled the poison-tipped spear Guran had given him.

The tip hit the lizard between its blind eyes. Then bounced off, to sink into the boiling stream.

"Didn't even scratch him," said the Phantom.

"Maybe we will have to turn back," said Karl. "Take our chances with the volcano."

"No way," said Gabe. "Listen."

A new roaring, bubbling sound was starting behind them.

"It's lava," said Jan. "Red-hot lava flowing into the cave. We can't turn back now."

The lizard continued to creep closer.

CHAPTER TWENTY-THREE

Barber, the fat owner of the Scarlet Cockatoo, pressed a concealed button in the shelving of the bookcases behind his desk. He was wearing a saffron-colored suit with a blood-red tie. A section of the bookcase swung out on a noiseless pivot, revealing a small air-conditioned radio room.

Squeezing his saffron-suited bulk around the case, Barber shuffled into the hidden room. He grunted, pushed another button, and was sealed up with the radio equipment.

He seated himself before the radio set, rubbing his pudgy fingers around the circle of his beard. While he waited for the radio to warm up, he said to himself, "Communications have never gone well on this caper. First I get cut off from McClennan. Now I can't even get a rise out of Silvera or Tinn. We'll give it another try." He spread his huge legs wide, sighing. "Sometimes I wish fate had made me more mobile. Then I could undertake field work myself. If only——"

The fat man blinked his tiny eyes and gave a surprised snort. A red bulb over the radio set had started to flash on and off. "Trouble," said Barber.

He cautiously shoved back his chair, turning toward the secret door. The red light could be set flashing by flicking various switches around the club. It was a danger signal, meaning somebody was bringing trouble into the Scarlet Cockatoo.

Barber placed one little eye to the peephole in the secret wall. A loud knocking began on his office door.

"Barber, open up! This is the police!"

The knocking continued.

"Open up, or we'll let ourselves in! We have a warrant!"

As the fat Barber watched the door of his office, it was forced open. Lieutenant Kiwanda of the Mawitaan police jumped across the threshold, pistol drawn.

Behind the lieutenant came Colonel Weeks of the Jungle Patrol, looking very angry. Then other police and JP men whom Barber didn't recognize.

Barber stayed where he was. Breathing very carefully, watching them fan out around his office.

"There's the bookcase Lemos told us about," said Colonel Weeks, pointing.

Lemos, thought Barber. So it's Lemos who betrayed me. This whole caper is going sour.

"If you're in there, come on out," called Lieutenant Kiwanda.

The left eye of Colonel Weeks, who was directly in front of the bookcase wall, seemed to be looking into Barber's eye. "Let's find the control button," said the Colonel.

A small wheeze was starting to rattle around in Barber's huge chest. He hesitated for half a moment, then punched at a button. The secret wall swung in. "Well, well, Lieutenant," he said as he stepped slowly into their range of vision. "You had better have all the right papers with you, and in perfect order. Otherwise——"

"We'd like," interrupted Lieutenant Kiwanda, "to ask you some questions about the Veiled Lady."

Wheezing, the vast man made his way back to his desk. "You want a travel agency, Lieutenant, or a tourist guide. I am neither."

Colonel Weeks caught his shoulder as he was about to sit. "No, Barber, we want you. If you talk now, things may go easier for you."

"Things?" The fat man broke away from the colonel and dropped into a wicker chair. His wheeze was growing worse. "What sort of things do you imagine I've done?"

"It may turn out to be murder," said the colonel. "Right now we've got enough to charge you with conspiracy to commit murder."

"Oh, so?" The fat man rested his palms on his knees. "Who is it I murdered, or planned to murder?"

"Me, for one," supplied Sergeant Barnum, who was leaning in the doorway. "Lemos was all ready to do me in on your orders. And maybe, though I hope not, you had Doc Love and her associate killed."

Barber fluttered his tiny eyelashes at the police lieutenant. "I'm afraid I simply don't understand any of this."

Colonel Weeks dropped both his fists down on the edge of the fat man's desk. "Try to understand this, Barber. Lemos has told us you arranged to have Gabe McClennan take over Doctor Love's flight. There hasn't been one word heard from that girl since she went down into the Veiled Lady."

Barber said, "It seems to me I've heard of this Doctor Love; I read an informative article about her in *National Georgraphic* or some such publication. She's a biologist, isn't she? Why on earth should I be interested in her?"

Sergeant Barnum walked across the office, straight

up to Barber's desk. "Because you got it figured Doc Love was really going in after the treasure of the Veiled Lady," he said. "You stuck your man Gabe with them and as soon as the treasure showed up he was supposed to let you know by radio. Only something went wrong."

"I really don't——"

"It's no use, Barber," the colonel told him. "We know you're in this up to your ears. Lemos has given us enough to put you away for a while. Your only chance now is to cooperate with us."

Barber sighed a wheezing sigh. He rested both hands on his broad chest. "Oh, very well, I'll be docile and helpful. What do you want to know?"

The colonel demanded, "What happened to Doctor Love?"

The fat man let out another sigh. "There you have me, Colonel. I know no more than you."

"Have you heard from Gabe since their copter entered the volcano?"

"Not a blessed word," said Barber. "He was supposed to contact me as soon as he could."

"Wait now," put in the stocky Sergeant Barnum. "You've got a couple of other heavies working on this job. I heard Lemos talking about them."

"He's been most valuable, hasn't he?" said the fat man. "Well, yes, as a matter of fact, I sent two more of my men to find out what had happened. Whether Gabe and the rest had died or whether that stupid spade . . . excuse me, Lieutenant . . . or whether Gabe had double-crossed me."

"Where did you send them?" asked Colonel Weeks.

"Eventually into the volcano."

"Into the Veiled Lady?"

"Yes. When I have my mind set on something, I persist."

"How did they go in?"

"By the same method employed by your Doctor Love. They used a helicopter," answered Barber. "It cost me a good deal to hire the blasted thing."

The colonel's head was very close to Barber's. "Have they communicated with you since they entered the volcano?"

Barber inclined one fat hand toward his secret radio room. "Not one word," he said. "I was about to try them again."

"Go ahead and do it," ordered the colonel.

The café owner huffed up, made his way into the radio room. The colonel and Lieutenant Kiwanda were close behind him.

Seated again at the radio, Barber made a fresh attempt to contact Silvera and Tinn. But no word came to him out of the Veiled Lady. With a tiny smile, the fat man switched to a new frequency. "Perhaps, Colonel, you'd like to hear what your troops are up to."

From the radio speaker came the voice of a Jungle Patrol helicopter pilot. "This is Sandy, calling the Llongo station."

"We read you, Sandy. What's up?"

"The whole damn mountain it looks like. Better alert all emergency crews to be on standby. We may have to evacuate most of the Llongo country around the volcano."

"Huh? Why?"

"Because the Veiled Lady is starting to act up, buddy. It looks to me from up here like she's going to erupt."

"Good lord," said Colonel Weeks. "We've got to get

135

out there." He spun around and ran from the hidden radio room.

Barber put his fat elbows on the table. "Well, there goes the treasure," he said as Lieutenant Kiwanda took hold of his arm.

CHAPTER TWENTY-FOUR

The Phantom said, "I think I see a way out." He looked from the gigantic lizard to the wall of the cave. "Doctor Love, shine your light over that way."

Jan did as she was told. "What do you have in mind?"

The great scaly monster was moving ever closer, its tongue lashing at the narrowing gap between them.

"The cavern widens up ahead there, just beyond our lizard friend," said the Phantom.

"Yes, I can see that," said Jan. "But how does——?"

"And there's a ledge running along the wall," continued the masked man.

Gabe was watching back over his shoulder, playing his light on the river behind them. "I can see the first wave of lava coming. We only got a few minutes between it and us."

"As soon as the monster stops being a cork in our bottleneck," said the Phantom, "as soon as the river's clear, move! Jan, you take my paddle."

"But what are you going to——?"

The Phantom crouched, then leaped. He went sailing over the five feet of bubbling boiling water between the side of the copter and the narrow ledge.

"He'll fall," said Jan, inhaling sharply.

"No, he's made it," said Karl. "Get hold of the paddle and be ready."

The Phantom worked his way along the ledge, moving closer to the great blind lizard. When he was op-

137

posite the enormous scaled head, the lizard became aware of him and swiveled its blind eyes in his direction.

"It's going to get him," breathed Jan.

The Phantom edged by the lizard, reaching the wider stretch of cavern safely. Turning now, he kicked out at the beast. "Hey, you!" he shouted. "Over here! Come and get me!"

Slowly, laboriously, the monster lizard turned. Its great long tongue began to whip at the dodging Phantom.

"This is like waiting for a drawbridge to go up," said Gabe, his eyes on the Phantom and the lizard.

"Over here, over here!" taunted the Phantom. "Come on over and catch me!"

The lizard hissed, its forefeet thrashing at the boiling water, which did no harm to its imperturbable hide.

"That's it!" encouraged the Phantom. "You've almost got me! Only a few more steps!"

The lizard waddled toward him.

"It's clear," said Karl, beginning to paddle.

"Now!" the Phantom called to them.

Jan, too, began using the makeshift oar with all her might. "What about the Phantom?"

"He said go," said Karl. "So we go."

"Boy, that thing gets uglier the closer you get," observed Gabe as they passed the giant lizard.

When they were parallel to its large snub tail, Jan said, "We can't leave the Phantom here, Karl."

"I don't believe he intends to sacrifice himself for us, Jan," Karl told her. "He must have something in mind." The current was flowing faster, pulling at their raft. "Though I'm having a tough time keeping the boat here."

138

The monster lizard had its head aimed straight at the masked man now. Its great jaws swung slowly open.

"I've had," said the Phantom, "about enough of you, old fellow." With a mighty leap, he left the ledge, vaulted over the monster's great gaping jaws, and landed smack on its scaly head.

"Hey!" said Gabe. "He's right on top of the damn thing."

The lizard's jaws snapped shut, catching only humid air. Its head started to turn.

Like a skilled tightrope walker, the Phantom ran, sure-footed, along the lizard's ridged back. Before the blind sluggish monster knew what had happened, the masked man had leaped again.

This time the Phantom landed square on the copter. "Okay," he said, "let's get going, people." He retrieved his paddle from the girl and took over.

"That was marvelous," said Jan. "I never thought you'd . . . well, yes, I guess I did think you'd make it."

"Save your congratulations," the Phantom told her. "He may get himself turned around and make another try for us."

"Yeah, he's starting to move this way," announced Gabe.

The swift current and the strong rowing of the Phantom and Karl quickly lengthened the distance between the raft and the monster.

As the scaly creature came lumbering through the water in their wake, it suddenly gave a high-pitched shriek.

"The lava," said Gabe. "The lava's caught up with him. We're going to get it next."

The Phantom turned his oar back to Jan, and then grabbed up a coiled rope. He rapidly fashioned a loop.

"Faint light up ahead," he said. "We must be nearing the falls. Gabe, grab the other end of this rope and make it fast to the copter."

Gabe did that. "Yeah, I can see sunlight up ahead. I hope we get to the sunshine before the lava gets to us."

Far behind them, the giant lizard cried out once more.

"Here we go." The Phantom threw his loop of rope, caught an outcropping of jagged cave wall, and tightened.

The loop held, the copter-raft jerked to a stop, yawing slightly, shaking in the tremendous pull of the down-rushing water.

Jumping from the craft, the Phantom landed on a wide ledge. "We're in luck," he told them. "We can walk along here." He'd brought another rope with him. Looping it over his shoulder, he helped Jan and Gabe up beside him onto the rocky ledge.

Karl was the last to leave the copter. "We're still a few yards ahead of the lava."

The Phantom jogged along the ledge. The cavern opened wide up ahead, a great hole in the mountain through which the boiling waters of the River of Fire gushed. "Yes, we're okay," he called back. "See, we can follow the ledge out this way and then climb out. That'll put us above the falls, clear of the boiling water. I thought I remembered seeing this ridge here when I was down below a few days ago."

"Can we climb down the side of the Veiled Lady from there?" asked Jan.

The Phantom said, "Yes, we should be able to."

He worked his way up along the ledge and out into the open. "Yes, we can anchor a rope around this outcropping of rock out here."

When they were all outside the cave, clinging to the rocky mountainside a hundred feet from the ground, Gabe said, "I never thought I'd be out here again. Boy, it's——"

Then came the most enormous explosion so far.

CHAPTER TWENTY-FIVE

Colonel Weeks paced the Jungle Patrol airfield while his helicopter was being readied. His pipe had gone out and he was swinging it as he walked, like a scythe. "Why did I wait so long?" he said. "We should have gone in after that girl the moment we lost radio contact."

Walking at his side, Sergeant Barnum said, "That's hindsight talking, sir. We had no way of knowing the Veiled Lady would go up. She's been dormant all these years."

"I suppose you're right, Barnum," admitted the colonel. "Still, I feel completely responsible for Doctor Love. If she's killed by this. . . ."

Barnum nodded at the JP copter. "They're signaling to us, sir. Let's go."

Striding across the field toward the ship, Weeks said, "I should never have allowed her to go down there in the first place."

Barnum stepped aside to allow the commander to precede him into the copter. "You shouldn't feel so paternal, sir."

The colonel frowned at him for a few seconds, then smiled a little. "I guess that's part of the job, Barnum."

Soon the Jungle Patrol ship was whirring up into the afternoon, leaving Mawitaan behind and heading for the Llongo country and the Veiled Lady.

"What's the latest on the volcano?" the sergeant asked the red-haired young pilot.

"They're moving everybody within a five-mile radius of the Veiled Lady," answered the pilot. "The whole country around there is suffering from earthquakes. Looks like she'll erupt for sure."

Colonel Weeks said, "Let's hope we get there in time."

"You're not figuring on going down into that volcano, sir?" the stocky Sergeant Barnum wanted to know.

"Huh?" blurted the redheaded pilot before he got control of himself.

"I'm not sure," said the gray-haired colonel. "If I do, you needn't worry. I won't risk anyone but myself."

Barnum decided to try to change the subject. "How about that Barber guy?"

The colonel was watching the landscape unroll below them. "What did you say, Sergeant?"

"I was speculating about Barber," said Sergeant Barnum. "The so-called mastermind behind the plot. What do you think of that treasure business?"

"It's hard to tell," said the colonel. "I suppose a fortune in gold and jewels could have been thrown into the Veiled Lady centuries ago."

"Barber sure believes in it," said the sergeant. "He's convinced Doctor Love went into the volcano to get herself the treasure."

"People with obsessions sometimes get to believing everybody shares them." The colonel tapped the pilot's shoulder. "See if you can contact Sandy or Smythe in one of our patrol ships near the volcano."

"Yes, sir," replied the red-haired boy. In a moment he said, "Here's Sandy, sir."

"Sandy, this is Colonel Weeks."

"I guess you know about what's happening here, sir."

"Yes, we're on our way out there to you now. How does it look?"

"Bad," replied Sandy. "Very bad, Colonel. Smoke is pouring up out of the volcano now—black smoke, yellow smoke. The whole peak is trembling and quakes are shaking up the whole countryside."

"I don't suppose," asked the colonel slowly, "you've spotted any sign of anyone inside?"

"No, sir. Sorry. Not a trace of Doctor Love. If she's still alive in there now, sir, well. . . ."

"Yes, I know, Sandy."

"There is one thing, sir. This morning a couple of teenage boys from the Llongo tribe came to the base to tell us they thought they saw another copter flying up and into the Veiled Lady."

"Yes, I know about that."

"What was it, sir, some kind of private rescue team?"

"Some kind of private hijackers," replied the colonel. "Any trace of them?"

"Nope," answered Sandy. "Like I said, all you can see now is smoke and more smoke. It's really shooting out of the old mountain now. And flecks of fire are showing up. It's like the biggest fireworks' display you've ever seen. Or maybe like the end of the world, with fire and brimstone."

To Sergeant Barnum, the colonel said, "We'll never get there before it goes."

"Doesn't seem like it," agreed the sergeant.

All signs of civilization were gone below them now. They were flying over jungle. Gazing down, Colonel Weeks said, "They say the Deep Woods is down

144

there someplace. And somewhere down there may be the Phantom."

"I thought he was just an ancient legend, sir," said the young pilot. "Isn't he?"

"The Phantom is more than a legend," said the gray-haired colonel. "I wish I had someone like him helping me now."

"Colonel Weeks," came Sandy's voice out of the radio. "Colonel Weeks?"

"Go ahead, Sandy. What is it?"

"The Veiled Lady is erupting," Sandy told him. Over the radio came a terrific explosion. "Can you hear that? She's spewing lava now; it's running down the side of the mountain. I'm glad we got the people out of the area in time."

"All except Doctor Love," said the colonel, slumping back in his seat.

CHAPTER TWENTY-SIX

The Phantom tested the rope. "You first, Karl," he said. "That way you can take care of any emergencies on the ground."

The four of them were huddled on the mountainside, clear of the sputtering falls which were beginning to shoot out lava.

Karl gave Jan a smile before starting his climb down the shaking side of the volcano.

The air all around them was a sooty orange color. There was a strong smell of sulphur.

Jan rubbed her eyes. "It's raining ash and rocks," she said. "Be careful, Karl."

The bearded biologist was twenty feet down the rope.

"All right." The masked man tapped the girl on her shoulder. "You next, Doctor Love."

"Shouldn't Gabe go?"

"I'm okay," the pilot said. "And the old rule is women and children first, remember?"

Jan gripped the vine rope, went over the side of the ledge.

When she'd descended a dozen feet or so, the Phantom said, "Your turn, Gabe."

"I can bring up the rear if you like," he offered.

"I'll do that."

"Okay then," said Gabe. "Here goes."

The explosions within the long-dormant volcano were growing louder and louder. It was like being in a city under bombardment. The air was thickening with black smoke; great flakes of ash and red-glowing rocks were falling everywhere. Tongues of flame seemed to flicker in the deepening blackness.

Down below the Phantom, Gabe coughed. He had already made it down ten feet of rope. Karl was nearly to the ground, Jan still some fifty feet up.

The masked man took hold of the rope and backed over the ledge. A few yards to his right scarlet-glaring lava was flowing out of the cavern they had so recently departed.

"Hey, look out, Doctor Love!" warned Gabe.

A flaming bit of volcanic debris had slapped against Jan's back. Her blouse was starting to smoulder.

"Hang on," said Gabe, "I'll put it out." He let go of the rope with one hand and was about to slide down to the girl.

The mountain gave a huge shake.

Gabe partially lost his grip on the rope. He fell.

"Oh, Gabe!" cried Jan. The flames were commencing to flicker around the blackened place at the back of her blouse.

"Don't fret." Gabe got hold of the vine rope after falling a half-dozen feet. It rubbed a wide raw welt across his palms before he slowed himself. He was now hanging only a few feet above the girl. "We got to get you put out."

Jan was trying to reach over her shoulder to swat the burgeoning flames.

Meantime the Phantom had been climbing quickly down the rope. He was at Gabe's side now. "Hold tight," he told the black man. The Phantom swung out around Gabe, dropping down beside the blonde

147

girl. Holding on with one hand, he slapped a palm against her back.

The flames died. "I feel as if I'm being congratulated for something," said Jan. "Thanks."

Karl was on the ground now. "You okay, Jan?"

"Yes." The girl let go of the rope, dropping the few remaining feet to earth. "Thanks to the Phantom and Gabe."

"It wasn't anything," said Gabe. "All I did was. . . ." His voice faded; his hands went limp on the rope.

The Phantom was on the ground next to Jan by now. "Look out," he said.

"It's his leg again. It's bleeding."

Unconscious, Gabe came plummeting down the mountainside from twenty-five feet up.

His feet firmly planted, the Phantom caught him in his arms. "There we go."

Jan said, "Let me look at his leg and——"

"The first thing we've got to do," said Karl, "is get away from here. Lava's starting to come over the rim up there." He gestured upward. "We've got to put distance between us and the Veiled Lady."

"The Llongo River is down this way," the Phantom told them. "We should be safe on its other side."

The three of them began to run, the masked man carrying Gabe.

From the woods nearby came the neighing of a horse.

The Phantom halted. "Hero?"

There was an answering neigh and the great stallion trotted out to greet him. Close behind padded Devil, the Phantom's gray wolf.

"They must have broken away from the Llongo chief to come looking for me," said the Phantom.

"Here, Doctor Love. Get up in the saddle, then I'll put Gabe there with you."

Gabe was coming to. "I don't need a pony ride," he mumbled.

Jan's foot hit the stirrup and she swung expertly up onto Hero's back. "No time for quibbling, Gabe. Get on board."

The Phantom helped the wounded pilot up forward of Jan. "Hold onto the pommel if you can, Gabe."

"Yeah, I can do that okay," said Gabe in a weak voice. "I can do that."

The Phantom patted his stallion on the neck. "Take them to the Llongo River and wait, Hero."

The powerful horse galloped off.

"You and I will run," said the Phantom to Karl.

"I hear jogging is good for you," replied Karl.

At the edge of the wide river, the air was not nearly as bad. There had not been an explosion from the Veiled Lady for several minutes.

"Maybe the old girl has quit showing off," Karl panted as he stopped beside the clear water.

"Hey!" Jan called to the Phantom. "We've run into some friends of yours."

She and Gabe had dismounted. Beached near them was a dugout canoe and in it were several of the Bandar pygmies.

Guran was on the shore, treating Gabe's wound. "This is a very ancient remedy," he was telling his patient.

Devil had been watching the little man at work. He turned now, and came loping up to the Phantom.

"Well, Guran," said the Phantom as he approached his old friend. "How do you come to be here?"

The little gray-brown man looked up at the Phantom. "I had what you call a hunch," he said. "A feeling that I should return here at this time. We had to slip by the Jungle Patrol, which was not too difficult, to get here, Phantom. They seem determined that all should leave this place."

"A good idea," said the Phantom. "Guran, can you take Doctor Love and her friends down to the nearest Jungle Patrol post?"

"If that is what you wish," answered the pygmy. To Gabe, he said, "Your leg will soon be well. Please climb aboard our craft now."

Gabe hesitated. "I don't know if I want to go back to civilization or not," he said finally.

Jan said, "Don't be afraid, Gabe."

"Yeah, but I was supposed to be working for Tinn and Silvera and those guys," said Gabe. "I ought to be turned in."

"No," said Karl, "you were working for us."

"Anyone who says otherwise," Jan told him, "will have to argue with us."

With Guran's help, Gabe rose to his feet. "Well, okay then. I'll come along with you."

Jan moved near the Phantom. "Are you going to be traveling with us?"

The masked man shook his head. "No," he said. "You'll be all right from here on."

The blonde girl bounded forward and kissed him on the cheek. "I'm glad at least one legend turned out to be true." She took a few steps back. "Will we ever see you again?"

The Phantom smiled at her. "Perhaps," he answered.

Karl reached out to shake his hand. "We can never thank you enough."

While they were climbing into the pygmy bark,

Guran came up beside the Phantom. "We will meet again in the Deep Woods?"

"Yes, soon."

"I am happy you have returned to us."

"As I told you I would."

Guran removed his thatch hat and rubbed at his head. "But I see you have discarded the magic spear I presented you with. Did you not need it?"

"I'll tell you about that back at Skull Cave," the Phantom said, laughing.

CHAPTER TWENTY-SEVEN

Colonel Weeks was squatting on the dusty ground. Beside him sat the plump chief of the Llongo tribe. The chief's face was smeared with ash; his plumed headdress was bedraggled and singed. Late-afternoon shadows fell across the two men as they talked beside the Llongo country Jungle Patrol outpost building.

"You know nothing of Doctor Love then?" the colonel asked.

The chief said, "I know only this, Colonel. She will return to you and her people."

The colonel's gray eyebrows lifted. "Why do you say that, Chief?"

"She will be delivered out of the flames of the Veiled Lady," answered the plump chief. "Indeed, that is why the volcano has exploded."

Controlling his temper, the colonel said, "What do you mean?"

"The great Ghost Who Walks could not get out any other way," explained the chief. "So he forced the mountain to explode, and blew himself out. Though I might wish he had arranged it so the lava did not flow across one hundred of my best acres of——"

"The Ghost Who Walks? You mean the Phantom?"

"None other," said the chief. "The Man Who Cannot Die."

The colonel glanced toward the post landing field. He was waiting for Sandy to return in his copter, so that he could get a firsthand account of things. "What makes you think the Phantom was in the volcano?"

Touching his fingertips to his plump cheeks, the Llongo chief replied, "Did I not see him with my own eyes?"

"Did you?"

"Yes. I stood as close to him as you are to me. I watched as he ascended the mountain and entered it."

"You mean to tell me," said the colonel, "that the Phantom climbed up the side of the Veiled Lady and he then went down inside her? That's impossible."

The big chief smiled. "For any but the Phantom."

Colonel Weeks stood up and began pacing in the long stripes of shadow. He drummed his blunt fingers against the side of his leg. "So the Phantom was in there, too?" he said. "Then he's probably dead, too."

"Oh, no," said the still-seated chief. "The Phantom can never die."

The colonel gestured at the blackened afternoon sky. "No man, ghost or otherwise, can possibly have survived what happened."

All at once the Llongo chieftain hefted himself up. "Listen," he said.

Drums were sounding, coming from some distance beyond the Jungle Patrol post.

"What are they saying?" asked the colonel.

Nodding, beaming, the Llongo chief interpreted the drum message. "The Ghost Who Walks has returned from his visit with the Veiled Lady," he said. "He has brought with him Doctor Love and two others."

"Where are they now?"

"No one knows where the Phantom is," answered the chief. "The lady doctor, however, and her two

153

companions are coming here. They travel the Llongo River at this very moment."

"Sergeant Barnum," the colonel called, "did you hear that?"

The stocky sergeant came running out of the post building. "What is it, sir?"

"They're alive, Sergeant," said the colonel. "Alive and headed for here. Let's get down to the riverside."

"Yes, sir," said Sergeant Barnum.

Guran handed Gabe a small leather pouch. "Apply this powder twice a day," he instructed, "morning and night."

Doctor Love, Karl, and Gabe were standing on the shore of the river. Behind them stretched a wide trail leading uphill. "The Jungle Patrol post is just up there then?" asked Jan.

The pygmy hopped back into his dugout. "Yes. You will be made welcome there," he said. "Now, farewell."

"Won't you wait and——?" began the blonde girl.

But the pygmy paddles were already knifing into the waters of the river. Soon the dugout was racing away into the fading afternoon.

"Well," said Karl, putting an arm around Jan's shoulders, "we're almost at the end of our journey."

"Yes," said Jan. "And it's too bad. . . ."

"Too bad?"

"Oh, I just mean—well, golly, in a way I'm sorry it's over. There was so much down there to study, so much to learn," Jan said. "Now it's all gone, finished and gone forever."

"I know how you feel," said Karl. "But remember, Jan, we were almost finished down there, too. If it hadn't been for——"

"Doctor Love, Karl!" called a familiar voice. "Are we glad to see you!"

"I guess," said Gabe, starting to drop back, "nobody's glad to see me."

"Wait now, Gabe." Jan caught his sleeve.

Colonel Weeks slowed, hesitating. "It's good to see you again, Doctor Love."

Jan smiled, ran ahead, and gave the colonel a hug. "Same here."

His face reddening, the colonel disengaged himself from the girl. "How in the world did you get out of the volcano?"

"You should have seen him the last couple of days," said Sergeant Barnum. "He's been worried silly. You see, he figured——"

"That's enough for the moment, Sergeant," ordered the colonel. "Let the lady talk. How did you get here, Doctor Love?"

"It's a long story, Colonel," the girl said. "In fact, you might even say it was a legend."

"Yeah?" said Barnum. "We heard it was the Phan——"

"Let's wait until we're all seated around a cool drink back in Mawitaan," suggested Karl. "There'll be plenty of time then for talking and explaining."

"Though even then," reflected Jan, "you aren't going to believe us."

After clearing his throat, the colonel said, "Doctor Love, I'm afraid I'll have to turn your pilot over to the Mawitaan police."

"No, I don't think so," said Jan.

"You don't understand," the gray-haired colonel told her. "He was hired by men back in Mawitaan to spy on your expedition, possibly even to kill both you and Karl."

Jan shook her head. "No, Colonel. Gabe was hired by us to help us get in and out of the Veiled Lady. And he did that, and a lot more than that."

"But——" said the colonel.

"This is another one of those things we can talk about back in Mawitaan," said Karl. "For now, Colonel, let me assure you Gabe is one of us and not one of our enemies."

The colonel looked from Karl to Gabe. "Very well," he said. "I get the impression you and Doctor Love know what you're talking about. Come on then. We'll see about flying you all back to Mawitaan."

"See, Gabe," Jan said quietly to him, "things will be okay now."

He grinned weakly. "Looks like, maybe."

As they moved along the trail Colonel Weeks asked Jan, "Another thing, Doctor Love, that's been puzzling me."

"Yes, Colonel?"

"Your last radio message to us. You said, 'Why it's a giant b——! What did that b stand for?"

Jan smiled. "Just that," she said. "A giant bee. B-e-e."

"What?" said the colonel, blinking.

"That's another of the things we'll explain later," said Karl.

"Boy, that's going to be some get-together," said Sergeant Barnum.

CHAPTER TWENTY-EIGHT

Sergeant Barnum's face brightened. He dropped the chain of paper clips he'd been fooling with back into his pocket. "Here they come," he said. Clutched in his right hand was a bouquet of white flowers.

"I see them," said the colonel. The two men started across the Mawitaan airport building.

"Here," said the sergeant, thrusting the blossoms toward Doctor Jan Love. "Sort of a *bon-voyage* offering."

Jan took the flowers. She was wearing a simple tan suit. Her blonde hair was pulled back and ribbon-tied. She looked fresh and rested. It had been three days since they returned to the capital. "Why, thank you, Sergeant. They're very pretty."

"I thought you'd like them," explained the stocky sergeant, "because the blossoms are so big."

"Yes, I've gotten used to largeness," said the girl.

Colonel Weeks said, "We've respected your wishes, Doctor Love. We've told no one the details of what you and Karl encountered down inside the Veiled Lady."

Jan watched his face for a few seconds. "I wonder if even you quite believe us, Colonel."

"Oh, yes," he assured her. "I believe you, but I'm wondering if——"

"The rest of the world would," said Karl. "Yes, Jan and I will have to think about this before we decide what to tell."

"Sometimes maybe," said Jan, "some discoveries are better kept quiet. I'm not sure yet."

Sergeant Barnum asked, "Where are you going next, Doctor Love?"

"Home," she replied, "just home to Boston. I feel the need of teaching a few very quiet, very simple, biology classes for a while."

Karl laughed. "She always says that. But I'll bet before another semester is over, she'll have plans drawn up for a brand-new excursion."

"I don't know about that, Karl. Maybe this time I'm really ready to settle down. I might even consider, well, we can discuss that when we get home."

"If you ever get back to Bangalla," said the sergeant, "come by and say hello."

"Of course," said Jan.

Karl cocked his head. "They're announcing our flight, Jan."

The lovely girl reached out her free hand, touched the colonel's hand, then the sergeant's. "Thank you both for being so considerate, and for worrying."

"By the way," said the colonel. "You needn't worry about Gabe McClennan. Lieutenant Kiwanda isn't going to charge him with anything, and the airfield is willing to take him back. After what you told us, Doctor Love, we're all willing to give him one more chance."

"I know," said Jan. "We talked to him in the hospital right before coming here."

In another moment, she and Karl were gone.

The pilot of the Bangalla Airways jet said, "Now, ladies and gentlemen, if you'll look to your right you will see the gal who gave everybody so much trouble a few days ago. They used to call her the Veiled

Lady, but I don't know about that. She seems to have lost her veils."

The great mountain stood out stark and black far below.

Jan took Karl's hand. "She doesn't look very formidable from up here, does she?"

"Distance is like time," said the bearded Karl. "It gives you a different perspective."

"It's sad," said the girl, her eyes on the retreating volcano. "All those amazing life-forms gone forever. And those two poor foolish men, Silvera and Tinn, dying for nothing."

"A good many people do that."

"What did Colonel Weeks say the name of the man behind them was?"

"Barber," said Karl.

"Yes, Barber. Imagine, we never even saw him and yet he played such a large part in our lives."

"I wonder if there could have been any treasure down there."

"I don't think so," said Jan. "The Phantom told me there was no trace of gold or jewels around the place of sacrifice."

"The Phantom," said Karl. "He was quite a fellow."

"Yes," agreed Jan. "And he's down there someplace." Impulsively, she leaned across Karl to wave at the window. "Good-bye, Phantom, wherever you are."

The jet roared through the sky.

Standing at the edge of the airfield was a tall stranger. He wore dark glasses, a wide-brimmed hat. With him, on a leash, was a large gray dog which looked much like a wolf.

The stranger's head was turned skyward. He was

watching the course of the Bangalla Airways jet that had recently taken off.

He kept his eyes on the plane until it was only a dot in the sky. Then, an instant before it left his sight, he raised his hand and waved.

"Good luck, Doctor Love," he said.

He reached down, patted the animal with him. "Come on, Devil. It's back to the Deep Woods for us."

The two of them walked away.